Woman Journalist

Woman Journalist

The Adventure of Village Virgin

Irsang Luther King

PARTRIDGE

To order additional copies of this book, contact
Toll Free 800 101 2657 (Singapore)
Toll Free 1 800 81 7340 (Malaysia)
orders.singapore@partridgepublishing.com

www.partridgepublishing.com/singapore

One

When twilight passes, night comes and lamps shine here and there. On a village is found a river flowing clean water. On the edge of river grows a shady tree which locates around villagers' houses. Underneath is the black shadow, it moves showing one's shadow, gets up and goes into house. Because highlighted by the lights, it looks a young woman with straight hair and white skin. She has interesting eyebrows because they are tapering. She looks thinking of something memorable in her life. What is haunting her reverie, no one knows the answer.

She doesn't come out of the house again during the night; she watches television, listens to music and reads a book. The remaining night is used for rest, she sleeps until morning. Waking up at 6 am, she then hurries showering and breakfasts. The food she enjoys only modest menu such as white rice, cabbage, and fried egg. After finishing breakfast, she sits back under a shady tree. This time, she is not daydreaming, but reading a local newspaper. The news topic she enjoys is journalism, she aspires to be a journalist. A moment later, her mother calls.

Elly, your phone rings, there may be good news from your friend.

Elly replies, okay Mom, please bring a cell phone here.

Based on their conversation is known her name is Ellysabeth, she is called Elly. Mother takes a handphone and gives. And it turns out the caller is a friend named Catheryna inviting her to leave village toward destination city, capital city. Catheryna who is called Ryna urges her not to continue to waste time just to daydream. And now is clear that her reverie is on her former lover while she was still in high school. Because of suffering from an illness, he has gone forever.

Ryna has left the village, they split up eight months ago when they graduated from high school. Ryna toward the capital to continue study in college while Elly remains in village stepping in English language course institution that exists. Elly knows English is supporting ability to work as a journalist.

Ryna's invitation affects her willingness to stay as a village resident. But she has to postpone to leave the village, she takes the months longer to ripen more English language skill. Her purpose becomes solid after four months passed. She thinks, if her language ability is still lacking, then when she had been in capital, she still has enough time to further refine it. Such opinion encourages her to consult with parents. Both parents agree toward her willingness to leave the village. It doesn't forget, two younger sisters pray to Almighty as a moral support to their sister to gain knowledge in capital.

Elly prepares documents related to departure. When the day arrives, they pray to God to ask for guidance at step she does. It is in the morning at 9:15 am, the entire family accompanies her to the railway station. Their way takes forty-five minutes. At the appointed time, Elly goes to capital, tears are unstoppable pouring out of their eyelid. Congratulations to my son on purpose that is the last her mother speaks at the departure terminal.

Arriving in capital, she goes straight for exit gate, a woman has waited for Elly in front of the door. And greeting sounds to call Elly from the crowd. She direct eyes towards the sound she has heard. A woman turns a faithful friend; she is Ryna. They talk friendly and Ryna invites her to rest for a while to enjoy light refreshment in the cafeteria. Elly orders an ice cream while Ryna asks avocado juice. They are a handful of minutes in cafeteria, then they call a taxi and get ready to go to Ryna's house. Because the atmosphere is quiet, taxi hurtles and arrives at destination matching to expected time.

Ryna now is no longer alone in that place, they become two friends settle in the simple and clean house. Because of being tired, they lay on bed. They get up from sleep when sun goes down and they are relaxed while watching television. Ryna remembers her past when she was still in a cool village with Elly. She then asks.

El, were you still thinking the deceased ex-boyfriend?

Elly is silent. Then she says, I remembered him when doing nothing, he was kind. Otherwise, I agree people's opinion saying the last experience has become history.

Oh well, you are better to plan a future; we hope God will give you the best way in finding a mate. Have you planned for future?

I want to continue a study, but now is impossible. Because I am waiting for the new school year.

Ryna suggests, while waiting for the new school year, you should deepen an English.

Elly nods, you are right, please help me find an English language course.

Ryna tells, you are better to join American Indonesian Institute, this course institution is much in demand by students. The next day, they hurry go to the course, its location is near from where they live. In front office is lettering: Please contact information. They approach a receptionist; she is a bespectacled middle-aged woman. Today is a good day, enrollment is being opened for regular class. Elly reads the registration need, takes registration forms and brings them home filled out. She sometimes asks Ryna who always accompanies her during filling out.

The next day at the appointed time, they return to institution course managed by professional workers. It is done placement test at the same day for each potential course participant. She is accepted at intensive class. On following days, she follows the course, back and forth from home to course and vice versa. Similar duty is conducted by Ryna who spends a time to follow the lecture.

Elly begins an adventure in capital. The first day of undergoing course falls on Monday at 9:00 am. She begins meets friends. One of them named Martha. She is young woman with black facial skin. Her showing is simple but attractive, she speaks politely. Another friend she knows is Darwis. He has white skin, an ideal height, and an athleticism body. This man is likely diligent for sport. His style looks like a movie star and his smile is charming. This guy shows nice personality.

According to a regular schedule, Elly follows the course three times a week. Relation with friends is more familiar. In a cheerful morning, her phone is ringing, she picks up it. From the phone's screen looks, a caller is a friend in course named Darwis. He asks for time to meet; she fulfills his wish. He comes with Martha. They sit on the terrace, speak a potluck, they may tighten the friendship. He asks Elly to follow the body fitness exercise. She agrees, and promises to join the sport.

The following week, he comes to pick up Elly to her house; they go to a physical fitness center, a place where he is used to spending the spare time. She sees Martha has come. After the exercise, they talk a story around the course, a story about family and career. The most interesting topic they are talking is a love story. They realize, men and women need love. On that occasion, he is offering a side job for Elly. He tells, the job can make money as long as worked well. Field she will handle is a public relation, it is a part-time job. As a village woman who is still innocent, his offer is tempting. She nods a head.

In the next exercise schedule, he goes back to her house. He has contacted her by phone, so she is ready awaiting. She gets in a car and they go to a physical fitness center. An atmosphere of emotion is welcoming, new friends greet her. After introducing themselves, they exercise according to each wish. Some athletes are riding a static bike, others are lifting the weight and pulling the spring. Participants feeling enough for exercise hang out at the cafeteria. One by one they then regroup and they are chatting.

She is young and graceful, this attracts man's attention. Robby approaches her. The information says he is a business leader engaging in the garment industry. It isn't too long; he joins them. His presence makes the atmosphere more intimate. At the end of their conversation, he asks her phone number and listing in his phone. The friendship between he and she is familiar, they prove by communication over the phone.

An evening after an English course, Darwis approaches Elly and whispers message from Robby. He hopes, she should get ready to be picked up at next Sunday morning because he has to come with Robby in getting together with entrepreneurs. Meeting will be held in the luxury hotel. She is proud because she will know many entrepreneurs. It is a good opportunity; she thinks.

Robby comes with the smooth car, gets down from the car and meets her waiting for him in front of the house. The pattern of life in big city tempts her. With pride, she climbs into a white car. Their journey finds no obstacles. In a few minutes they arrive at the destination, a cool and luxurious hotel. They sit in lobby, guests are passing. After waiting for minutes, she asks,

Robby, when does the meeting take place?

We wait a minute, the committee will come soon.

They spend half an hour waiting, but signs of the meeting among garment employers are unclear. She asks the next question.

Robby, when does the meeting takes place?

If you cannot stand, we are better to wait in hotel room. You stay here; I have booked a room for us.

Robby's words make her remembers the tale of life in the big city. She wakes up from temptation that might tarnish her purity. She says I won't deign to stay at the hotel. My opinion says, man and woman are worth entering the hotel room if they are not a coupled of married. He is upset, stops the step and approaches her again. He sits next to her and shows dollars.

Elly, put this money into your purse, let us tandem at the hotel.

What do you mean?

I want to make love with you.

She is conscious, a devil's need wants to trap her. She rebels and hurries. From the front of the hotel, she walks the meters and stops a taxi. She tells the driver to her house. Getting out from taxi, she steps up in a hurry. Ryna looks at Elly and asks what has happened. Elly talks at length friendship with Darwis until she did know Robby, the man who would destroy morale and dignity of her family.

The first examination has passed. As close friend, Ryna advises to be careful in men, Elly muses. Elly at first guessed Darwis to be a god of helper for her future. He turns out a toxic to life.

Two

Time goes by so fast, four months have passed, the new school year comes soon. Elly no longer thinks friendship with Darwis. That experience makes more open-minded. She is aware, the temptation in big city worries. If she is not careful, she will meet problems.

She is soon to find out university admission. Although she has a year of graduating from high school, but she has a high spirit to continue study to university. The field of study follows her ideal is journalism. In addition, parents hope, she has went to top university. Her intelligence is never doubted. Of the three universities she has idolized, they issue the same result; she passed with satisfactory grade. The parents suggest she chooses a state university. A new era of her aim begins.

She studies on campus that is a top-rank university. The pattern of learning in university differs from while she was still in high school. To reach a good achievement, she has no choice but studying hard. She has no problem on the living expense. She asks for cost of living in moderation, never thinks an excessive life. She realizes knowledge is basis of a person to achieve success; it is much more important than anything. Therefore, she plans to finish university on time.

Approaching midterm exam, she gets a call from family. Mother advises her to return to village soon. Further message states that her father is ill and is in hospital. She is shocked and dazed to know father's health. Beside facing new challenge, her money is not enough for cost of returning to the village. Ryna is a friend in need. With little comment, she says,

Ryna, please help me!

If I can do, I would help you.

Please borrow me some money for fare of back to the village, my father is ill.

Oh my God, I hope your father recover soon.

Ryna concerns on friend, she takes out money and hands on Elly. Thank you friend, Elly says while in a hurry getting ready to leave to railway station. Ryna is not willing to let her close friend in sad alone. She helps Elly prepares all needed. Time is on leaving, they hug as a sign of togetherness. Ryna then says goodbye and be safe to reach the destination.

Elly leaves according to fixed schedule. Air temperature inside the train is cool. She reads a book because she will face midterm. Circumstance of her father in hospital makes her concentration disturbed. To expel feeling of worry, she tries to contact mother by phone.

Hello mom, how are dad now?

Father's health hasn't improved.

Father was tired, where are you now?

I am now in train heading back to village.

How is your condition, are you in good health?

I am all right; we hope dad recover soon!

Don't forget to pray to God.

She is now quieter. At least, father's health is not getting worse. She rereads a book while keeping diverts concentration. Through train window, she enjoys surrounding landscape. Before arriving in vicinity of village, farm life is even clearer. Rice plants decorate whole place around it. Village life dazzles when looking at the palm trees keep waving as wind effect.

Palpitation of heart quickens when the train she is riding has reached destination. Her presence in hospital first time meets her younger brother who at once cries and hugs her. She then asks,

Where is mother?

Mom is in treatment room with dad.

Next, they go to place where father is lying. Mother is bowing sluggish, she gets up from chair and embraces Elly with emotion. As a sign of sadness and longing, without realizing they shed tears. Atmosphere of sadness makes father wakes up from sleep. Seeing Elly is in front of him, father smiles and gets out of bed. Her presence turns out to contain particular strength for father's health. It is possible; he has missed on eldest daughter who becomes foundation of parents to set an example for the younger two. Only two days she accompanies father in hospital. The doctor advises, he gets enough rest at home.

It differs from an earlier when Elly was still in the village, now she no longer daydreams under the tree. She stays at the home to spend time with learning. She does nothing to serves sick father, mother understands her busy, mother handles solely father's care.

A week passed, her duties in the village are just learning and preparing for an exam. Exam schedule leaves only three days away. Father who has been healthier advises her to return to capital that day. If return is in haste, it could be tired and affects the concentration when facing the exams. Good suggestion of a father, she returns to capital.

Health of beloved father has continued to recover, it makes her more comfortable. She arrives in capital early afternoon. She applies regular and keep continuous learning. This pattern makes her never learn until late at night. As usual, she goes to bed around 23:00 pm, that is a time setting she does.

On the cheerful morning before the day starts an exam, she is awakened by sound of alarm that has been arranged before going to bed. That time shows 05.30 am. She showers, changes clothes, has a breakfast and goes to campus. There is nothing to bother her mind, she undergoes exams with full concentration. She is confident of getting good grades for subjects taken. Exam period ends for a week more. Important moment lives a need, waiting for exam results announced.

She inspires those supporting a career later. Brilliant idea appears, she figures out how to write an article in the print media. She tries to write a short article on education, its title is a good way of learning. She spends her time off to complete writing. She was fascinated and smiled after completing the short work. Next she thinks where she has to hand over it. Her mind is fixed on People Media, a mass media in village in which her parents becomes subscription client of it. She thinks, who knows her work can be published. The parents read and they know the author. She works an effort toward it. A case may happen, People Media rejects her work. So she also sends his work to other publishers. Now she is relaxed waiting for the exam result and answer from the mass media editor.

Waiting shows result, exam announcements occurred. Her performance was satisfactory. Taken subjects passed with above average grade. She has a next duty, looking for an answer on her writing, no news she gets. While waiting for this one, she returns to village gathering the whole family. Father is healthy, so she has nothing to do except helping light work like cooking, ironing clothes, watering the flowers. She never forgets to read magazines which present day life duty.

The sun is rising in east, father is sitting on terrace. He gets a dish of hot coffee from wife. And trader of newspaper comes in front of the house. Father gets up and takes newspaper clipped to the fence. He watches the news keep emerges, no hot news, everything is the day-to-day life. She opens new page; she is surprised, excited and cynical. Without realizing, father screams while calling Elly.

Elly, come here first, I read an important news.

What is it?

Look at this newspaper, your name is listed as an author. Is this right?

Yes, the work is my article.

Father is happy for her achievement, he hugs her with emotion. A moment later, she gets a warm welcome from mother and siblings. As a sign of early successes, parents take her to eat at restaurant.

Her success as a writer in local newspaper raises prestige in village. After eating at restaurant, the neighbors welcome her with congratulation. They flock to greet her while uttering the same word, congratulation and successful.

This achievement is still average, but for most people at her age, it can at least encourage spirit to reach higher goal. She gets new energy injection, her fighting spirit is up. She remembers old magazines; they contain some interesting articles. Mother informs her magazines were stored on a bookshelf. She takes two pieces from its place then both are slipped into a bag containing clothes. Because the plan, she will return to capital tomorrow morning.

It is drizzling in the morning, this causes her plan delays for a moment. Ten minutes passed, drizzle stops, and she rushes to the railway station. She remembers magazines, takes one of two magazines brought. The journey to capital she travels for forty-five minutes, she spends thirty-five minutes in reading. She got new inspiration on how to write good news.

Three

Journey from village to capital without hindrance, she came home without a flaw. Ryna greets Elly. They shake hands and embrace with great familiarity. Ryna knows People Media publishes Elly's article. For friend's achievement, Ryna doesn't forget to congratulate her. You are still teenager but you have been able to make an interesting article in mass media, Ryna says with smile. Thank you, Elly responds fun statement of friend. She opens a briefcase and pulls out a tiny meal bought while she was still in railway station in village. She invites Ryna to enjoy snacks. They dissolve in relaxed chatting until dusk.

A week ahead of national holiday, Elly intends to spend a time with a visit to tourist place. She wants to breathe fresh air and intends to find inspiration to create new article. To that purpose, she invites Ryna to attend. Ryna has nothing to do, she fulfills Elly's interest. Be they go to tourist location. Residents call it as Cool Air Region. They pick place to relax in small shop in highest position of the region. They want to get the answer why people call Cool Air Region. Based on information from shopkeeper, the origin of the name is according to the condition of local air. It is true; the air is cool. Another question they want to know is why local tourists visit this place, but no one gives satisfactory answer.

They then move to another shop, order the same, fresh and warm drink. Waiter meets customer demand, she serves two glasses of sweet tea before them. Ryna takes a hand phone and plays songs in it. The music sung by the well-known group of musicians airs around the place. Elly is lured by music, she shakes a head. Single men approach, their eyes lead to Elly and Ryna, someone interests in Elly. He casts a warm smile on her, but she is still cool. He doesn't get a response; he comes over and introduces himself. His name is Wolter, he is final year student at a college. Their introduction only lasts a dozen minutes. Elly goodbyes him and invites Ryna to visit a discotheque. Elly's wish to visit discotheque invites for Ryna's question. What Elly wants to enjoy? Ryna at first believes to avoid Wolter and friends. She gets the answer once they are inside the discotheque. Elly says, a wish to visit the nightlife just wants to know what people do on nightlife. She intends to make writing on what night women do. Elly's explanations are understandable, but it still leaves another question. Ryna doesn't stand sitting in discotheque because she is anxiety. They are young women and nobody accompanies them. Ryna issues the questions.

Elly, you are so desperate to visit this place?

What happens? A tourist location is safe enough for any visitor.

But nobody accompanies us?

Don't worry, this place is available security officer.

Are you sure?

Yes.

Ryna's fear vanishes, her feeling is now safe and fresh. They watch on entertainment while chatting with waiter, sluts are passing in front of them. Elly takes a pen and notebook. She notes the important things useful for writing. Her attention on life around it stops when watching Wolter and friends come to location. Wolter sees her and approaches. Their communication fixes on agreement to meet again in capital.

Their visit to Cool Air Region was over, Elly and Ryna have even set foot in capital for a week. Elly received incoming calls from Wolter, they were recorded in her phone memory.

She opens a message saying Wolter is wishing to visit her. The time listed in phone showed the wish has not been done. She is awaiting his presence. She hopes to see good acquaintance, but she fells eager because of experience when traveling with Robby. Her waiting happens, he comes on Monday afternoon after she attends a lecture.

As a more junior student, she expects guidance from him. It happens, he talks final project he is working. According to him, he was doing research on live of female sex workers. The results mentioned various reasons women plunge into sex servant. Women say because of life's trials, others give reason for having been hurt by man. Most are curious, they gave reason to make much money. She becomes more interested in his visit because his research hasn't completed. She wants to visit a study site, but her heart still saves a question who is this man?

Next visit occurs three days later. He comes by wearing jean and T-shirts to blue-tinged color. The meeting answers questions whom he is, his parents work as lecturer in college. Another information says that both his parents are active in various spiritual event. Her confidence against him grows when he asks her to attend religious service. The event is scheduled to be held next week and his parents will attend.

Spiritual day arrives, Wolter comes to pick Elly, and they set off using a dark-colored four-wheel car. There are several pieces of compact disk in car containing spiritual songs. He inserts a disk into musical instrument, and the hymns echo in car. The music fills the silence during the journey.

They find group of people when watch shows 18:15 pm. It is a sign they soon arrive at the destination, a simple hotel with large parking place. Thus makes the driver has no trouble to park a car. They walk to the meeting shortly after he parks a car.

Visitors are crowded, they are adults, two of them are married couples. He invites her to meet them. He salutes and shakes hands with them and afterwards introduces her. She is still wondering whom the parents are. Before event starts, he tells her the couple are none other than his parents. Her introduction with his parents convinces her he is well educated man.

Her meeting with him was unexpected, she hopes he shows a kindness. So, she suggests the need to allow her taking part in helping research. He agrees and promises to tell her when the time comes.

On the following days, they communicate more often. He visits her when he has a spare time. One time on Saturday morning, she receives phone call from him. He asks where she is now. The answer states she is relaxing at home. He expects that she goes nowhere because he wants to come home at once.

He gets home as promised; the time shows at 10:00 am. Ryna steps to meet him. Sit down please, she welcomes. Further, she says, please wait a minute, Elly is still in the room receiving a call from parents. He steps into terrace and sits on available seat. Elly talks no serious discussion, parents are a mild longing. Wolter and Elly meet after phone disconnected.

Hi Wolter, how are you? Are you waiting for me?

Just the minutes, Ryna said you received phone call.

Ryna was right, mom contacted me and said she missed.

A mother cares for son. So, you become a mother, you must find a mate.

His statement makes them laugh together. He tries to chat dating because he has been crush at her. To reach an intent, he pays special attention. He hopes his attention will affect her understanding against his turmoil.

Four

Wolter shows behavior to protect Elly, it makes her fascinates him. His parents work as a lecturer, they are a noble people, these help her believes him. As a village woman, she has shortcomings. She needs kind man with enough knowledge, so he qualifies to become a tutor. She thinks Wolter meet her expectation.

To get more data on the end task, he intends to conduct added research. He fulfills promise, contacts her by phone. She will get a guidance on articles she will write later. As a more junior student, she wants to make him as a helper for college counselor. The plan, he will conducts a research a week later.

He has several times research; the right time is a relaxing day, it falls on Saturday night. He comes to see her the minutes before leaving, guides her so she doesn't let a step at a challenging location. If one goes wrong step, danger will happen.

Briefing on her ran well, it spent thirty minutes. An expected time arrives, they go to study site. They only find a bottleneck, so they arrive at destination as planned.

The first place they visit is the security post. Their need is reporting to local security officials they will research. Security officer asks a woman with him. He explains that his friend is Elly, the person on duty to help conduct research. Report is completed, they do the task.

The researcher task is looking for data related to goal. At a specified moment, he intends to find out women's history working in that location. He suggests her to wait a moment in a resting place and then sees a pimp. She amazes to see a male she has ever known. She could not believe that a person she sees is Robby. The man approaches her.

Hi Elly, do you still remember me?

Are you Robby?

You are right. Do you receive a visitor today?

She confuses dealing with a philanderer man. Don't make mistakes, so Wolter ever conveyed the message. She sighs as she whispers words, oh my God, forgive sin of this man. After saying those words, she is away and contacts Wolter by phone. He soon comes and meet Robby.

Hi friend, can we help you?

I come not to ask your help, but want to have fun with Elly.

She is here to help me.

Go bitch, don't be a hero. I now don't need researcher.

Blasphemy committed by Robby makes Wolter offended, fisticuffs can be prevented. The security officer relays misunderstanding that occurred. Calm has been restored, Robby passes while Wolter and Elly are back doing their job.

A quarrel has happened interfere with Wolter and Elly research. The remaining time available they use to interview two women only. They then say goodbye to security guard and rush to leave location. They don't return home but stop at a small shop under the shady tree. In that place, they enjoy light refreshment while talking valuable experience they have had. On that occasion she tells experience when traveling with Robby the time ago. Wolter is amazed. He doesn't forget to give advice on her to pray to Almighty. Further, He leads her to go home.

No woman expects ugly experience. But, such cases are common happen in every major city. Challenges and trials come and go. Sweet seductions are accompanied by Satan's temptation. If someone cannot block, the future could be smashed to pieces.

She knows the rigors of life in the big city. She is careful to steps and makes a friend. Ugly experience is a teacher for life. Her nature becomes more mature and adult. Her preoccupation in improving the knowledge leads to time passed. She has a year living in capital.

On a particular night, she wakes up from sleep; the time shows at 24.00. She remembers television broadcasting news at midnight. She turns on television and chooses a channel. At once it looks great news of battle of the two countries involved the war. A journalist is suspected of working as a spy, he suffers inhumane interrogation. In addition, it broadcasts a journalist who has been tragically shot dead. The news she watched at the night makes her doubt to go working in journalism. She muses, she is thinking of a journalist' load in performing the duty. Musing takes her asleep on the bed.

Fear is still haunting her mind when waking up in the morning. Then, she daydreams for a moment, remembering bitter events experienced by journalists while covering war news. Is it realistic to stay aspire to be journalist? This view is inherent in her mind. Her phone rings when she is anxious and full of question mark. Incoming call comes from Wolter, he intends to visit her with aim wants to see her welcomed. She is happy, she can discuss with him on her worries.

She greets his presence. With little time, she serves bottle tea before him. Further, she asks for opinion on him a plight duties of a journalist; she focuses a question on joy and sorrow experienced by war correspondent. He advises if she later continues journalistic work; she doesn't cover the war story. He adds, other areas are interested, such as economy, science or technology. His opinion make her eager to learn the journalism.

Hard-fought at first, getting a success then. This expression makes her tough to face the earlier trials. She will achieve a good performance when continuing a talent.

She is now working on articles related to bitter experience faced by journalists when covering war story. She collects experiences, trials, temptations and torture. If processed, the result may be ten folio pages. She writes a script and asks him which serves as faculty mentor. Based on data she collected and his guidance, her work leads to article of eight folio pages. And, putting a work to print media.

A month later, the leading print media publishes her work. She gets information through him who is a paper's subscriber. Two days later, she, with him visits the publisher office. Company's manager hands white envelope containing a sum of money as reward for work. On that occasion, she receives an invitation to take part in competition to write a story on electronic mass media. She receives and asks permission.

They spend little time at her home; Ryna joins, then go to location around five hundred meters from home. Their destination is small restaurant, students come here. When they arrive at scene, Ryna at once asks questions.

Why do you invite me to this restaurant?

He replies, Elly won an achievement. She awards sum of money. So, she invites us to eat together.

Ryna answers, well, that is surprising, thank you, you may always be successful.

Their conversation doesn't run long, it only takes fifteen minutes because the waiter serves their food menu message. This idea the first time they do, so they enjoy with pleasure and joke sounds between them. Togetherness is closed after Elly pays an accounts listed on billing statement.

The following days Elly spends for reading. Besides reading lecture materials, she doesn't forget to prepare for writing competition organized by the electronic media. She invites him to judge. So, he is back and forth to her home during two weeks.

On following days, she must fend for herself, as he must go abroad for a purpose related to the final project. She is talented and never hopeless. Even without his presence, she continues to prepare to be the best in the competition. The manuscript was completed; she hands it to organizer committee, delivery is at registration day. Thrilling moment comes, waiting for announcement of competition results.

Expectation arrives after a month of waiting. The results are announced on Saturday night at 19:00 pm. She comes to dress in simple clothes, half hour before show at start. There are crowds, they are participants. Her heart skips a beat ahead of event in open. Dak, dik, duk, heart sound vibrations so for minutes. Towards 20:00 pm, honored guests come up on stage, they will announce who is the best at the event.

Her heart subsides after hearing the jury decides she is a winner three. She is grateful to God for her achievement. Most audience around her are greeting and they congratulate to her, including from friend, Ryna attending with her that night.

Five

The competition was finished; the results were announced. She has questions. Where did Wolter go? How long has he lived there? Does he meet me again? Could he be with me? God knows the answer on her questions. She remembers her habit in the past, daydreaming. Change has occurred. She drives reverie with reading and writing. If God will, he sees her again. She now surrenders to God. Whatever she does, wherever she goes, God determines.

One day, the weather is cheerful and airy; she takes a time to visit the bookstore. The goal buys a book presenting a way of writing. She is cool to sort out the source of reading. A man named Jordan accosts her.

Hi Elly, how are you?

What is your name? She replies.

Oh, I am an admirer of you; I knew you when watching television which broadcast writing competition a time ago.

From the brief conversation, he admitted that he knew Wolter. They lecture on the same major and department. He explains that he is looking for guidebook to prepare a thesis.

The meeting continues with chatting in the canteen on the second floor of the building. It becomes a silent witness to where Wolter went. And it turns out he had an important task, he went to neighboring country, Singapore. The goal was to escort his father who suffered from heart attack. Jordan says, Wolter will soon return to homeland if his father recovers. It is said that he once told Jordan that his lecture will soon be completed around two months later. I hope his father recovers soon. That is the last sentence she pronounces to finish their talk.

They often communicate by phone. One day, he contacts her intending to meet. She doesn't mind, but because she has a business, she refuses and promises to receive his visit when she has time to spare. He is curious. The next day he tries to contact her by phone with the aim wants to ask her when she is ready to receive a visit. The phone is not active. He sends a short message. It has just come in after she activates a phone an hour later. Her answer says a day after tomorrow, on Sunday morning at 10:00 am. Her certainty makes him pleased. He is still single; he visits her to the house. Ryna is being relaxed sitting on the terrace. She rises from chair and steps to approach him.

Who do you want to meet? She asks him standing right in gatehouse. I want to meet Elly! A moment later Ryna enters a house and tells a friend. Elly, someone is waiting for you. Elly rushes out and greets a guest.

Hi, how are you, Jordan?

I am fine? I hope you are too.

Take a seat please!

He pulls out a chair and sits across from her. From inside the house, Ryna is peering from a slit, she wants to know who the handsome man is. Oh my God, he is handsome, Ryna thinks as stepping and sitting in a chair in the middle of the house. In that place, she sits with relaxed to watch television. Her eyes toward television but her heart and mind are still focused on him. A few minutes later, Elly goes into the house for a particular purpose. Ryna calls her and says,

El, come on here!

What happens, Ryna?

Who is that man?

Friend.

Friend or boyfriend?

He is my friend.

Please you introduce him.

They are out to meet Jordan, and talk something on the terrace. Be their three friends speak campus life and love. Now and then they laugh together when he mentions love at Elly and Ryna. The important case, Elly doesn't find out in love with him. She says, Jordan is no more just casual friend, she still hopes Wolter. A woman who hopes for Jordan's attention is Ryna. So, she is more active to respond any opinions he expresses. She interrupts the conversation by asking for his phone number. He meets her wish and conversely; he records her phone number. Be Ryna a friendship with Jordan. She sends various limericks through short message service to attract his attention. Rhymes hit deep inside his heart. The rhyme is,

I am staying up all night, I am waiting for man.

Three nights I could not sleep, thinking the inside my heart-Jordan.

This poem captures the heart and makes him a moment of reflection. He wonders who is a target shooting whether Ryna or Elly? The answer is more directed to Ryna. Jordan has a view, Ryna and Elly should receive fair sevice. No harm if he gets closer to Ryna. His interest in Ryna doesn't make friendship with Elly away. But even their friendship is getting closer, Elly's closeness with Jordan reinforces his closeness with Ryna. Ryna is confident that Elly won't bother her friendship with Jordan. In addition, their parents are close.

Ryna had closeness to Jordan. When he came to meet Ryna, Elly often asked him questions related to writing. Ryna understands while he is wise to serve. An older people should be a role model for the younger one. He has no preferential treatment at Elly. The friendship between them runs well, they find nothing. For each visit, he first contacts Ryna by phone. One day, he comes unannounced at Ryna; she is out of the house. Elly accompanies him talk on the terrace. A few minutes later, Ryna goes home and catches Elly and Jordan cool joking and laughing. Ryna is suspicious, she scowls. Without throws greet her friend, she strolls straight into the house. Her nature is strange. Elly and Jordan are surprised. Elly follows Ryna into the house and explains the fact. Ryna receives Elly's explanation but still keeps a sense of suspicion.

The friendly relation between Elly and Ryna be stiff. The next state to be frozen when Ryna witnesses Elly is receiving a phone call from Jordan. You are a traitor, she mutters as closing the door loudly. Elly is upset, disconnects the phone with Jordan then walks to meet Ryna.

Ryna, why are you not friendly?

Why do you say that?

You closed the door loudly, there might be something wrong with me?

I hope you understand me!

Are you jealous?

It is up to you!

Elly doesn't want to hurt a friend, she understands Ryna is falling in love. Elly responds Ryna's jealous, she keeps distance against Jordan. Jealousy makes their relation becomes less harmonious. Ryna first lived in rented house they occupy, Elly understands it. So, she must give way and she weighs to seek new rented house. While doing her task as a student in university, she has asked friends new residential she needs. This information flows from one person to another, it reaches ears of Jordan. Elly's plan to seek new residential becomes a question for Jordan. What is the main reason she wants to move? He contacts her by phone.

Elly, where are you?

I am at home.

Jordan further asks the purpose she was looking for new shelter. She is reluctant to explain; she worries it will add to the problem. But she assures he will understand why.

She cuts off discussion with him. Such a manner makes him wants to know what happens. After taking a car key, he rushes to drive to largest speed and arrives in front of the house. The scenery around the house looks different from usual. The fence is closed, no front seats. Impression suggests disharmony inhabitants. He knocks the fence. Someone is moving a step toward the window. She draws the curtain and peeks outside through the existing narrow gap. Knowing Jordan has been waiting outside the fence, she comes out. She opens the door and throwing a smile at him.

How are you, Ryna? he asks to welcome her.

I am fine; she says as opens the gate.

Where is Elly?

This question makes her stun for a moment, she finds difficult to answer. He can detect a condition when witnessing her who remains silent when he asks the same question. Well, now is chaotic circumstance he thinks. With a soft voice, he asks her willingness to be kind to call Elly. That way is successful persuasion, Ryna goes into the house to meet Elly.

Elly, Jordan is on terrace, he hopes you meet him.

Okay, I see him at once.

Elly steps out of the house onto the terrace and meets Jordan. He can detect stiffness that occurs. He knows there has been a misunderstanding between Elly and Ryna, their friendship must be repaired. They met at the tavern. He later gives meaning to Ryna how his friendship with Elly. Ryna is conscious, and she sheds tears as a sign of grief on a mistake.

Elly, forgive me, please!

Well.

They both later embrace to express forgiveness. They solve the case, the friendship intimates again. He afterwards delivers exciting news to Elly stating that Wolter will return to homeland next week. The news is an important case for Elly because she will soon meet with her idol man. He presents a good plan by inviting Ryna and Elly to pick Wolter together to the airport. Both agree and they plan to leave an hour before the plane carrying Wolter landing.

Six

Awaited day arrives on Friday afternoon. They leave at 15,30 pm, Ryna sits in the front with Jordan, Elly is on the back. He is controlling steering wheel of Japanese white car equipped with air-conditioner. Cool air in car contributes to cheerfulness on the way. A trip to the airport spends an hour. They arrive on scene the minutes before landing. Bulletin board notes the plane carrying Wolter will land fifteen minutes later.

The remaining time is a minutes, it cannot be used to enjoy light refreshments in the cafeteria. So, he invites friends standing in front of the exit. Visitors are flocking around them.

The minutes later, passengers have stepped out of the airport. One of them is a young man with a thick mustache and his hair is cut. Jordan waives a hand toward him, he greets with a helping hand, then they shake. Please get acquainted with them, Jordan quips while directing his gaze to Elly and Ryna. Wolter wonders, how Elly and Jordan at the airport. He has never communicated with her, he is curious and asks Jordan.

Dan, how do you know Elly and Ryna.

It is a long story; we discus next time. How is your father health?

He is healthy!

A minutes later his father and mother appear. The close relatives attend at the airport, they greet his father recovering from an illness. His mother reflects when staring at Elly's face. She looks to wonder a woman in front of her. Elly approaches the mother and shakes her while mentioning a name. Oh my God, I remember now. Did you ever attend worship services with Wolter? Mother asks Elly. It is true; she replies with emotion. Mother nods and smiles. Further, Elly shakes hands with a father who looks thinner than usual. They spend less time, each group returns to the car and leave people pride airport.

After two days passed, Elly gets a text message from Wolter which expects her willingness to attend an event on blessing to cure Wolter's daddy. The plan, they will hold a blessing event on Sunday evening at 17:00 pm. I am okay; she says on the invitation. It makes her heart flowery. She hopes that her presence can create close relation to both of his parents. She hopes everything goes well.

A day before the event, on Saturday at 17:15 pm, Wolter, and Jordan, comes to pick her. They want to enjoy the fresh air around the capital. Today is a good day, the sky looks clean with no sign of rain. They set out to use red car owned by Wolter, sit in pairs and heading to the supermarket. It looks Wolter wants to shop something related to the event. In supermarket they visit place selling cakes and bread, sort out snack, next meet cashier to pay cakes and bread they need.

Wolter's light duty finished. They go to canteen luxurious and decorated with colorful flowers and nice accessories. They enjoy a soft drink and talk with familiar while joking as if to prepare themselves on the show tomorrow. Several weeks have passed, it makes them want to spend time by talking young people including thesis and work plan after finishing a lecture.

Time goes by, Wolter looks at his watch. It turns out they have spent over two hours. He shows a cue to friends with the purpose so they leave the canteen. They move, he is at the forefront directing his friends walking to find the parking place. He takes a key to the car, starts the engine, depresses gas pedal and drives away from the supermarket.

The cars are not as crowded as weekday, the car they are traveling speeds on average. During the trip, Elly asks Wolter's plan after studying. She hopes he finds a job matching to his field. But, the answer she receives is less according to what she expects. He says, after having won the title of scholar, he doesn't work soon, but he intends to continue studying to abroad. She stuns for a moment. If he goes abroad; it means soul mate is far; she retreats for the next few years. She hopes God gives her a way.

At the time they arrive at the house, Elly and Ryna get out of the car, wave goodbye and thank you for a kindness. They walk for a few steps and get ready for a shower. After hanging out in front of television, they go into the bedroom and sleep until morning.

Today Elly spends time for studying, the next she does the same. She gets to learn to write when having a free time, never spends in vain. Thus is her routine every day. A week passed, next week comes true, thus continues from day-to-day. A troubling comes, time for Wolter to undergo thesis exam is getting closer. It means the parting stays a matter of weeks

On Sunday afternoon, he comes to visit her, next they go to Mall. They drink a moment while talking her progress in writing. She says, she is interested in continuing to explore writing. Because, she aspires to be a good news writer. He supports her goal and promises ready to help when she needs. She is silent as realizing that he is no longer with her. She asks questions.

Why are you so eager to support me?

It is a noble job.

Are you sure want to leave me?

Why do you say that?

You will study abroad soon.

I am not abroad forever, one day I will return to the homeland

When do you get a test?

This Saturday.

Next Saturday stays a few more days after which he goes abroad. Loneliness fills her mind, she will part with him soon. Who else guides me? She thinks as looking ahead. Her thought is interrupted when he says, Elly, don't forget to pray for me on the day I take thesis exam. Okay, she replies to respond her idol expectation.

The seconds go fast, a minute passed. Several minutes pass, it spends an hour. Thus, time passes. On Saturday morning, she prays for her lover success. She awaits the crucial moment of the thesis exam result which he lives. After the middle of the day, she gets a phone call telling he graduates with honor satisfactory. On his success, he invites her to meal at the restaurant. This invitation is a happiness, and she is getting ready to wait for him. Because of traffic congestion, he arrives at her house twenty minutes longer. In the restaurant they visit, she shows cheerful face. She has a restlessness. It is reasonable, his success further clarifies their parting moment. She doesn't want to dissolve in anxiety; she asks him.

When are you planning to go abroad?

She keeps silent for a moment, then she asks again.

Well, will we soon part?

Yes.

Where do you go to continue study?

To England, I will go next month.

She is less excited to eat a delicious dishes available in front of her. She enjoys rice, vegetable and side dish is fried egg flavored with enough sauce. They are silent, no question and answer. They are waiting for leaving the restaurant. He calls the waiter and asks how much he should pay the bill. He completes the proposed bill by removing pieces of paper money. Once everything is sorted out, they leave restaurant then return to her house.

She at home is thinking the best to do later if he goes abroad. She tries not to be immersed in grief. The lecture should complete as the need. She prays so God meets her expectations. If the goal is reached, she will continue to follow support skill writing.

She accesses a website; the challenge arises. It asks each person who gifts writing to propose short story manuscript containing what students do outside the study time. As the organizer needs, she types manuscript as much as five-page folio. Work is bound and sent to the organizer, a well-known tabloid magazine. Two weeks later she gets good news from the editor. The company asks her come to office to receive honor as reward.

The success adds to the optimism sense. She is active to deepen the knowledge in writing. What she is thinking is planning to write a novel, but she doesn't find an idea of an interesting story. To reach a goal, she is looking for inspiration from various sources such as friends, newspapers, magazines and Internet.

Though she has dug information, but she hasn't found an intriguing idea. As long he is still in homeland, she contacts him by phone. Oh, I have an interesting idea to write. Just wait there, he advises her. An hour later he arrives and suggests an interesting idea. Elly, if you don't mind, I suggest you to write big city temptations. Next, he outlines the story summary. Wow, your idea is interesting; she replies. She picks up a diary and records various importance spoken by him.

He excuses in woman he adores at the last meet. She smiles and shakes hands with him. The message is, if you are successful, don't forget to tell me. It is sure; he says. She stands in front of the door and waves as a sign to release sincere lover.

Seven

Does Elly become sluggish since Wolter went to abroad? The answer is no. Does she become lonely since her boyfriend left? It is yes. Is her capacity to summarize a novel blunt because he doesn't guide her? The answer awaits result.

She reopens notes in diary. The story starts from beginning of summary written when told by him. She writes masterpiece. A page of folio is complete to be typed, it continues to next page, so she does. She stops writing before work is completed thirty folio pages. When the lecture is off for two weeks, she seeks source of inspiration for writing. A solitude is a main choice. For that purpose, she returns to village. It is more quiet, most villagers have to go wander. The people living in the village now are elderly people, they spend time in the old day.

The dark comes, a sign of night has arrived. She is waiting for the moon rising; it shines. A beam of light from outer space lights up most Earth. It takes part in adding to the quietness.

She sits under a shady tree in front of house where she used to brood alone. This time she is not brooding, but she looks for source of inspiration for work. She makes brief note, its model is author's work containing most of novel story. She stops scratching a pen for a moment, looks at nice full moon and thinks distant lover in land. Work continues for an hour, she then goes into the house to fill stomach rumbles. Reverie reoccurs when she returns to shady tree. She watches the full moon faithful to light up the Earth. Oh, this moon is amazing, her heart whispers as she starts again to work. The environment is as though inside the library, no annoying noise except cricket pealing specific sound.

Quiet and silence atmosphere make her cool in work. She realizes time is late at night when dew drops. The mother is out, and she tells Elly to take immediate go into the house. Let soon mom, my task soon be completed. Twenty minutes later she gets up and goes into the house.

Even though time is late at night but it doesn't make she stops working. She picks up a laptop and types part of the story she wrote in a diary. Mother is stunned to watch her tenacity. Kid's love is a long pole, otherwise, mother's love is along the way. So says proverb depicts mother's affection toward son. Mother offers warm milk to support the capacity of Elly's work.

Elly, I prepare a glass of milk for you, okay?

Okay mom.

Mother presents a glass of milk on a table. Thank you, mom, she says to the woman who gave birth to her. A typing job stops at the time television broadcasts night news. As a woman who is studying in university, she never misses interesting news at night. There is no important news. She turns off the television, goes to the rest room and sleeps.

The rest of holiday is no longer, it stays ten days. She uses free time to work. Early in the morning, she sits on chair typing manuscript. She thinks of the stories. Her mind focuses on Wolter's message. When she was with him, he promised to deliver story ideas over the Internet. She opens the Internet, a hope comes. The man she loves has sent a message through her account. The content is the brief description, and it needs to turn. Oh Wolter, you pay me a big enough concern, God may always bless you.

Her work is unfinished, it is still a quarter section. She walks to view. Journey stops somewhere under a palm tree that grows on the riverside. She takes the phone and activates the strand songs in it. From there she steps to another location, the distance she goes only takes a few minutes. Her step stops in a wall of the building part of a small sluice. The air is cool, its surrounding is growing shady trees, they can protect a person from the sting of the sun. She sits on the wall and looks at surrounding environment. Her feeling stuns watching teenager woman passing the village not far from her. A woman upholds basket where goods are laid. Work shows her nature never gives up, and she has high morale. There is the green and nice environment. These describe the state of the good personality of villagers who aren't greedy, so they still protect the environment. New experiences bring new ideas. She no longer goes further. Her decision is to return home to cultivate new ideas into the form of a story.

She prefers staying at home to finish work at remaining time. So novel has now reached a half part of the entire plan. Last day in the village she uses to visit Ryna's family. It is a long enough since they last met; it causes deep longing. When she is just standing in front of the house she heads, a woman in fifties rushes from inside the house. She knows the guest; they hug once the door is opened.

Elly, how are you?

Well mom, where is dad?

He is drinking coffee. Wait a minute, I call him.

Ryna's father comes soon and greets Elly. When seeing Elly is standing in front of him, the father thinks of her daughter, Ryna.

Elly, how are you?

Oh, I am healthy.

Does Ryna experience many problems?

Oh, we always face problems, but those are still within the bound of reasonableness.

Well, I hope you are protected by Almighty.

Father invites Elly sits while mother steps into the kitchen to prepare a glass of hot tea. They sit in a living room talking the village, residents and village youth job now. Mother tells village residents who discuss Elly for a success in competition the time ago. The villagers said, she was village star, because she could toss the good name of the village. Praise to the Lord, she says on mother's story. The mother opens photo album containing pictures of she and Ryna when they were the children. She laughs at because she remembers her childhood which was cute and full of happiness. At the end of her visit, she receives a white envelope containing money to be handed to Ryna. Father, mother, I take my leave she says while leaving the house of Ryna's parents.

She has finished a work. Most materials are as notes, they haven't been typed, she will bring them to capital. She leaves the village in the morning and gets ahead of destination city before the sun stands upright on the Earth.

Ryna gets news saying Elly has returned to capital this morning. Ryna has been waiting. She steps closer to Elly when she sees her friend gets out from the taxi. Ryna welcomes friend who has arrived. They shake hands. Ryna ask, Elly, how are you? I am superb, Elly answers to the question. She opens a bag, takes white envelope and hands over it. Ryna tells gratitude and steps into inside the room to store the surrogate she has received.

Elly is still eager to work, she prepares herself to write. Diary is issued, a laptop is opened, and she turns on it. Her fingers are in action typing writing materials brought from the village. She only stops when lunch time arrives. She orders lunch pack and eats at home. That day, lunch is closed by tasting papaya.

She has a good enough experience, writing job she does is more smooth. Her mind as to have been filled with a computer program, she is easy to get a good story idea. Fingers work, it causes her work was nearing completion. Before ending the novel story, she intends to contact Wolter to ask more opinion. She accesses the Internet, opens an email account and writes a message to him.

In the modern era, most people search for information through the Internet channel. He opens an account, an incoming message was sent by Elly. He types a summary for a story and clicks a send button. A moment later, the comment on-screen says message has been sent.

She wants to finish the job to write a novel. She accesses the Internet, opens an email that comes in and reprinting the story idea coming from him. Her fingers move to type source of the story she has got. Oh, I will turn hundred more words, and I finish a novel. The end of the story needs little time to work, it only takes twenty minutes. Thank God, You have to belong during writing this novel.

On information from various sources, she offers her work to a publishing company. If she is successful, the results could help with the costs of daily life including paying tuition purposes.

The novel has finished to work. For a time, she is no longer thinking of writing but concentrating on learning. She is optimistic her work will get a serious response from a publisher.

She wakes up from sleep after midnight; she feels the sunlight goes up to the bedroom. At that time is night. What she experienced was a startling dream, whatever it means, no one knows. She is trying to figure out dream's meaning. She hopes the dream is a good sign as praying to God. After praying, her restlessness loses and she lays on the bedroom.

Ryna comes out of room in the morning watching Elly is sitting on a chair in the living room. She greets her and says, Elly what are you thinking? Don't think of a theatrical life. Elly smiles. She asks Ryna to sit nearby, then tells a dream that happened last night. Ryna is trying to gauge a thought. It is a positive sign, your match is close, or you will get a windfall. These sentences make them laugh together. She afterwards leaves for college. Elly's reverie continues the minutes. She hurries to shower and goes to campus.

In the afternoon, Ryna arrives first at home. She gets a letter inserted through the bottom door; the sender is a publishing company. Its location shows around the city center. She takes the letter and puts it on the table, then sends a short message on Elly. Elly has just finished a lecture, she responds the message by going home.

Elly, this letter is for you.

Thank you, Ryna.

Elly receives a letter. Her heart is flowery knowing the sender is large and well-known publishing company. A letter is opened and read. Oh my God, I get success she says after reading it. Elly, what is your success? Ryna asks on Elly's statement. The next Monday I am asked to come to the editorial office to sign contract agreement on my novel. As a sign of emotion, Ryna hugs friend while banging her back. You are greet, Ryna says to respond a success achieved by Elly. Thank you, friend, such is the answer on praise. Thank to God. For a success, she asks Ryna to pray together to thank Almighty.

Elly, and Ryna, come on Monday, Elly will sign the contract agreement. They arrive twenty minutes before the appointed time. They wait in the lobby for minutes. A staff comes to meet them and asks Elly to face with law department, an authorized party handles the agreement. In that place, she reads the terms and conditions offered by the company. I understand, she says to the law manager. The cooperation agreement is signed soon on paper stamped.

Before leaving the signing room, she signs a receipt for a sum of money. It is an advance payment of part royalty. She smiles when receiving money and meets Ryna in the waiting room. Later, they contact Jordan. Hello Jordan, Ryna reaches him by phone. He is relaxed and picks up the phone. On that occasion, she tells Elly's message, so he meets them at the restaurant which takes ten minutes from office location. He agrees and they meet at promised place. They eat ordered food while the bill is settled by Elly.

Elly knows that her success is inseparable from parents' support. So, she calls to the village and contacts parents after arriving at home. Her mother is shocked and proud of achieving the eldest daughter. Father is amazed to hear the conversation between Elly and mother. He is curious, and mom, let me do the talking. Mother hands the phone to the husband. Talk between Elly and father begins, it happens the minutes. At the end of their conversation, father says, if you do well, mom and dad will be a long life. Dad doesn't forget to tell, so she is not arrogant and is always humble despite achieving success as high as the sky.

Her success is inseparable from joining Wolter who gives her a help. She opens the Internet and to thank you for his kindness and guidance during doing a work. May you be in good health and you get success in each work, such is her closing message to him.

Eight

In young age, Elly has won several brilliant achievements. Her work ranked third place in a competition, and her novel will be published. She thinks incomplete if she doesn't achieve a degree. To achieve a goal, she visits the library.

Business to learn makes her forget the time. Time goes fast, four months have passed.

Time to receive royalty has arrived. She is in need of money; she goes somewhere that provides automatic teller machine; available near the campus. She attracts a sum of money. The question comes to mind; she is surprised, on the machine screen states account balance. From where the funding source is. Did someone make a mistake in sending money? She takes a home key from the purse and opens the door. When opening the door, she sees a letter found on the floor. She takes the letter and hopes fun. It is notice of novel book sale and royalty that has been transferred to her account. The royalty exceeds the cost of living for the next year.

Elly earned an extra income, her spirit is buoyant, new ideas arise in the mind. She wants to take part on brief training in journalism. She remembers an announcement she has read the newspaper. Its content invites anyone interested in studying journalism. She visits bookstore intending to buy a newspaper; media where most announcements and advertisements covered. There have lined up several prominent newspapers. She sees, none of the newspaper containing information she needs. She moves to another location of the store. The steps halt at place providing information for each visitor in need. Good day mother, she says to the woman on duty. She asks a work.

Mother's suggestion asks her to visit the central office of journalists. She is amazed to crowds there, most visitors are undergoing training.

Participants queued. She signs up for the next group. She fulfills an administrative form, including the registration fee payable in cash. Next information says the training for the new group will begin on Monday during five days starting at 16:00 am until finished.

Elly is a woman who upholds discipline, so she never comes late. On Monday, she comes half an hour before the training begins. Participants arrive, they are more than 80 people. The participants enter the room where the training is conducted. Seconds before the training starts, participants have entered the room. The list of attendance is running, recorded participants are 95 people. When training takes place, the room is closed, no one is allowed passing over and again in the arena during the training period. Participants are needed to turn off the phone.

Registered participants come from various backgrounds. There are university students, fresh graduates, a part-time journalist even people who are unemployed take part. During training takes place, she focuses, wastes no time. When question and answer session takes place, she gets serious attention from an instructor teaching. The instructor in charge is senior journalist handling war coverage. He is male sex named Alex. Alex says, Elly is a talented woman, she has the potential to be a great journalist. Her talent looks when she asks a question. She speaks politely and has a systematic speech while her question is sharp and focused. In addition, she shows mature personality. Although she is still in the twenties but her behavior has shown someone having over thirty years old. Alex has a strong intent to reach her, but he is still waiting for the right moment. Time arrives, the last day Alex teaches. Once training is complete, he contacts the administration staff to ask for her address and phone number. It is easy, administrative staff fulfills a wish.

At noon on the third day of training, an administration section named Louise contacts Elly by phone. Louise asks Elly come in an hour before training begins. Elly gets information saying that Mr. Alex wants to talk to her. It easy to fulfill, she comes within the promised time; she meets Louise.

And, Louise invites her toward Alex's workspace in the room equipped with air-conditioning. Alex is ready to welcome her arrival.

Good day Elly, how are you?

Well, I am happy to meet you.

They shake hands while Louise gets out of room and returns to her desk. The conversation take place between them. She gets an offer to work in print media where he becomes a journalist. She rejects the offer, her study is not completed yet. Their conversation reaches a light point, she is received as a part-time worker. The job is helping senior staff processing news materials that go into the editorial desk. He considers, part-time job is a temporary target. The main target is she in time will become permanent employee recruited to work as a journalist in the company.

Besides good luck, she receives an award from journalist institution. She is declared to the best second of participants. For this achievement, she gets an appreciation plaque as evidence she has followed journalism training. Sentence printed on plaque states she is the best second participants to ninety-five people contributing to undergo course organized by news hunters.

Print media where she works as the part-time employee is one of three major company in capital. It named Voice of People. It is daily newspaper underlining public opinion; it focuses to matters on the interest of small and oppressed people. Her presence in daily Voice of People is running well. Besides earning perquisite, her experience helps to increase knowledge. It makes her personality grows more mature.

One time when she does a part-time job, Alex meets her before the lunch break. He smiles while stepping into her room. A senior journalist greets her with the sentence, Elly, could you to my room! Welcome, she says as she follows him step toward the fifth floor of the building. He first arrives at office room followed by her seconds later. A secretary to him welcomes her into boss's room. The room is decorated with modern style, the war coverage photographs are hanging on the wall. These show the covered events occurred abroad, it may charge a memento during covering of the deadly war.

Elly, do you have plenty of time to spare on the next Sunday? She answers, it depends on what we do. If I have an added job, I try to prepare a time. Tomorrow I will be out of town attending economic expert meeting. I hope you can go with me; he convinces subordinate. Oh, I am ready for it; she says to meet call of duty. They promised to go from office; she arrives twenty minutes before the appointed time. Because only a day trip, she only brings a small bag containing enough clothes. She dresses casual clothes in blue jeans and white T-shirt striped red. It is suitable for a white woman as her. They are escorted by a driver. The destination is fifty kilometers. Nice natural scenery looks when they will arrive to the destination, the blue beach looks nicer because the surrounding grows palm trees. Her eyes goggle to watch the interesting beach.

They arrive an hour before the event starts. She interviews important figures. With deft, she notes the important words spoken by interviewees, work is well and it runs. She stops covering the story at afternoon. He tells her to get ready for dinner at a location near to the event takes place. Driver escorts them to a restaurant serving typical of local food. She keeps weight, so she eats in moderation.

Twilight passed night comes, but Alex has shown no signs of going home. He invites Elly to move into a hotel next to the restaurant. They have a chat rumors occurring many artists. He intends to gain time. The hotel's television has shown time at 21:00 pm. She wonders his behavior, she asks,

Mr. Alex, what time do we return to the capital?

Why should we rush home? Task of covering is finished!

Tomorrow I have to attend class.

I have attended college, it could have skipped.

His answers are strange, those looks as uttered by a slacker. Her suspicion grows when she asks again. His answer is inconsequential. He takes her to stay with him at the hotel. She refuses. He threatens her with the following words, if you are not willing to belong at the hotel, I leave you here and I return to capital alone. The threat makes her silent. A moment later, he pulls her hand, seduces while uttering words of seduction. She refuses because she is determined not to give up her virginity to a man who is not her husband. No, Mr. Alex, she cries and releases the hand from him. He threatens, Elly, you should be aware, finding a job is difficult now. If you are not willing to serve me, I fired you. She looks weakened, he back holds in smooth hand and says, come on honey, I need you. She struggles and pushes him when she will be embraced. You are a lecherous man; she cries as in a hurry to leave the hotel.

Atmosphere beyond the hotel is quiet, now is showing at 22:30 pm. There are only traffic cars belonging to residents. The night air is cool due to coastal air is blowing through the surrounding neighborhood. Such circumstance invites fear on her. But where she has to complain, no one resident comes up before her.

The night is quieter; the waves roar sound louder while the sound of water splashing beach adds to her fear. She ventures to cross the street, stops at the bus stop, and waits for transport. No transport passes, but a smooth dark blue car flashes before her. What is a woman standing alone at night, the driver thinks while watching her standing confused. He stops the car and moves backward toward her. Hi sweet woman, what are you doing standing there alone, he is calling. The car occupant thinks that she is waiting for philanderer men who become customers. She is silent, even she looks away keeping her gaze away from the idle man. He with friends get out and approach her. She fears and steps away. A herd of men chase her. Her heart is pounding, she runs to avoid wrong intents of unscrupulous men. She heads toward locate fishing settlement. The step halts at houses of fishers. Fear is still happening, she turns to back to find out whether she is being followed. She screams for help when witnessing black man steps toward her. Fishers hear a shout, they at once surrounds her. He is a local resident because of run out of cigarettes intends to buy to a small shop. The rowdy atmosphere doesn't continue, a prominent fisher comes and speaks with her. Her heart is still pounding, she tells the whole experience until arriving at that place. The fishing village is home to communities far from immoral behavior. Citizens are polite toward the women. She is accommodated overnight in a home until sunrise. A resident then delivers her to freight terminal by using a motorbike. The man gives her secure sense; he escorts her to the city transport to be set. He gets off the transport after the driver signals for leaving. She smiles at him, waves and says words, may God repay your kindness.

She has returned home. The incident which would disfigure her virginity is stored in her mind. Alex is immoral man, no time to meet him. His behavior makes her not to work for three days. She won't believe in him although he holds a key position in the office.

She should be wise in employee status. Coming should get a permission, going should leave a message. She puts a letter of resignation in sealed envelope and delivers the personnel department. The letter is handed and excused for not wanting to meet with Alex.

She has twice experienced male poor treatment, experience is a good teacher. Noble values running in the village still survive to this day. She won't receive any bids that must sacrifice moral values, let alone have to sacrifice her virginity. She is now concentrating on finishing the study.

Nine

Time flies, she has undergone three years of university. She will have a certificate that can be used for work. Wolter, her male lover who has achieved Master's degree is in the homeland.

He changes after returning from abroad. He is being reluctant to talk dating problems. This was disappointed. Age is enough, he has enough science, but no sign of getting married. Questions store in her mind. Is he serious on me? Has he had a new girlfriend? Or his parents don't approve of their love affair?

He is a real man and has noble personality. His parents work in education, they are active in various religious event. So he may not pretend to fall in love, let alone playing a woman. She several times met with his parents, no sign of the parents not to agree. Their behavior was friendly, welcomed and educated. His coldness is only in matters of love, friendship with her is still going well. He is always ready to help and guide her whenever needed. If she wants to share the experience with him, he comes to give various opinion. She is eager and hopes for his love. But she is worried because no clarity when she will be married.

The wish not to marry appeared when studying abroad, he was suffering from the disease. Doctor's examination said, there were abnormalities in blood. What disease he suffered? No one tells. But as those men who suffer pain, he knew what disease he suffered. The argument was reasonable. He didn't want a woman he married suffer later. His behavior makes her curiosity. She tries to find out the answer. A way is extracting information from his close friend, Jordan. He tells unsatisfactory information. He convinces her Wolter didn't have a new girlfriend.

Elly is upset as her close friend will get married soon. Ryna before was in village expressing to parents an intent wants to marry Jordan. Both parental brides approved that plan. The wedding will run three months later. Preparations related to that happy day were being run. Elly invites Wolter to attend a wedding. It is risky invitation because he doesn't want to raise expectation on her. She will hope the same expectation. Her companions know that she has had a handsome and wise boyfriend. Her insistence is met by him, they set out together to attend a festive wedding. When they are in place where the wedding takes place, she says,

Wolter, they are happy, don't you want to get married?

Just be patient my dear!

Who will marry me?

A man who loves you!

What is his name?

God knows!

That answer makes her reluctant to talk dating, she prefers being a friend.

Mate is getting far, sadness comes. Amid her seriousness completes the study, less exciting news comes from village. The news is delivered by text message. Father is ill and laying in hospital. Trial is heavy, it makes her stamina is getting weak, her mental collapses and her mind digresses. Is this so-called social justice? Is God fair? Her steps are weak although she may travel to village. As usual, she uses the fast train with affordable rate. She is silent during in the train thinking whether Almighty summons her father. She hopes God extends his life.

The hope is fulfilled, he still breathes when she arrives in the hospital. She sees he is laying weak. He smiles at her; it makes her comforted. Mother tells news stating he is suffering from dengue fever, and the doctor may not restore the health. Mother has cautioned the possibility of her tuition will be disrupted.

He had a week treated in hospital. His health is worse, it causes he is moved to intensive care unit. According to patient data at the hospital, most of hospital patients treated in that room gave off the last breath. Five days later, father receives same fate, his eyes are closed as a sign of peace has passed away.

Daddy....., Elly cries loudly as crying and hugging body of the father laying dead on the bed. Crying continues as watching her two siblings standing and weeping beside her. Tears subside when hospital medical staffs approach them to express deep condolence on the loss of her father. Warmth with the father is over, fond memories are unforgettable. Father is buried in the public cemetery. After the religious ceremony was over, they leave burial site at afternoon before sunset. Goodbye dad, we hope you are received within loving God.

Post-burial of the father, Elly discusses with mother, her siblings involve. Their talk focuses on continuing her study. Mother argues, if her study continues, then they should stay in rented house. Heritage house must be sold to pay for her education and to finance the needs of her siblings. Over the past few days, most of mother's savings has been drained for cost of father care. Mom, I hope our house doesn't rush to sell, I will try to find a job to pay for my living cost, that is her suggestion on the mother. Mother nods with the tears because she is sad after her husband left. We hope your aim can be accomplished, mother says encouraging to the daughter.

In her savings account is listed balance enough to cost of life till six months. At issue, she has to think of contract costs alone. Since Ryna got married, she now stays rented house alone. There is no bright idea of doing that can meet demand. Her mind is fixed on publishing company in which her work has been published. The next day in the morning she goes to that company. She expects on the way to the company, her wish can be fulfilled.

She meets financial manager. The point is explained, the manager contacts marketing department. Thank you for God, sale statistic proves her writing is interesting to readers, its sale is satisfactory. The company meets an expectation. She gets a loan enough to meet her need. The load of her mind is looser, the cost of contract has been available.

A month passed, a new challenge arises. Mother hopes that younger brother lives with her in capital. She suggests so mother's hope is canceled while waiting for developing a better life. The suggestion is received.

To explore new ideas, she intends to be a newspaper customer that includes advertisements. She asks newspaper agent, so she is every day delivered newspaper called Daily Capital. There is no problem, the merchant agrees, and she is asked to fill out the subscription form. Administration completes a few minutes.

Now is a Sunday, she becomes a customer of Daily Capital. The newspaper is available when she wakes. She opens the main page where hot and interesting news are presented. She next opens an advertisement page, watching every column where advertisements are listed, no job offers matching her ability.

I hope, companies offer a job for news writer. Several days passed, no company offers a job. Hope just emerges after she subscribes to newspaper for three weeks, but that is less follow her ideal, only women magazine that wants to load short story on daily.

Ah, the job is still writing field; she sends job application. A company asked applicants have to send a letter of application over the Internet. She accesses the Internet; she presses the send button, an application is sent. Now she is waiting for announcement from company that promises to do it as soon as possible, either through electronic mail or mobile phone. Two days after sending an application, her phone rings as a sign of incoming call. The caller is unknown. She picks up the phone and connection begins. Her heart is pounding after learning the caller is staff of women magazine which opened job vacancy for writers. She is asked for interview that will be held on Tuesday morning starting at 9:00 am until finish.

In the scheduled day, she wakes up at 5:00 am, heads for the bathroom and pours freshwater into the body. The water temperature is cool adding fresh of her body in the morning. Finished bathing she eats breakfast dish comprising a slice of bread and a glass of fresh milk. Then she sets up files. Preparation is dozen minutes. By using light-colored shirt and gray skirt she goes to the office of women magazine with a taxi. She arrives at location the minutes before an interview. The minutes later, she is called and sits on the available seat. Interviewer team has known her. Good morning woman, have you appeared on television, is it right? An interviewer asks her. Another interviewer stars at her as opening resume. Another says your experience is good after seeing a resume.

Experiences and accomplishments she has achieved are encouraging of work available, so questions are not too difficult to answer. The record shows it only spent fifty minutes. The day is a good news; a publisher receives her as a writer of short story published each week.

Besides following the lecture, she writes a short story that has been ordered. She has satisfactory writing talent, so in a relaxed, short story needs three hours for completion. The honor is low; it is useful to help a daily life. Payment is cash, paid a day after her work published.

Company's schedule decided, work will be published as much as four times a month. Royalty she gains is satisfied and is more than a month living expense. Income has now increased, she ventures to meet mother's expectation the time ago calling her younger brother to capital. He soon follows through life in big city. She picks up him to railway station and they get back together to her house. If she is before joined by Ryna, now she is with her own biological younger brother. He has a different talent to her. His name is Bernard, he has a talent to trade. So, he aspires to work in marketing.

Ten

She has been four years to set foot in capital, her study has entered fourth year. Soon, she will prepare final project, a thesis, a necessary for the student to say graduating from university. Although it is not the right time to write, she has squared off to work on it. She needs help; she calls Wolter. They promise to meet in campus where she attends the lecture. He arrives around 10:00 am, and she has finished attending a lecture. Her heart pounds at sight he comes up before her, she loves him. They were together during four years, the end of love is difficult to answer. However, they are still good friend.

She intends to write a thesis related to television journalist. He supports and suggests her work should not contain risks, but more focused on domestic politics. His suggestion is good, she accepts. He even promises to give data and reading materials related to work plan. She looks at last duty materials although her lecture remains eight units of credit. These will be completed two months later. This week is an important moment for the learning progress, she is waiting for the exam results. The estimate doesn't fumble, her performance is satisfactory, getting the highest value for fields of remaining study. Since then, she completes duties to follow a lecture, the remaining is a final assignment.

First day of the month she spends to write short story manuscript. A second day she does the same. Three days later she studies for the final project preparation. A week of remaining time she uses flirting with a boyfriend. On that occasion, he suggests her to prepare a thesis outline as a precondition. She has had data; she finds no obstacle to prepare an outline, taking three days to complete the work.

She suggests an outline to guide lecturer; a senior professor who is an expert in social, economic, political and humanitarian. He has received news he will get her visit. This is exciting news for the bald-headed man. He gets news saying she is a smart and talented young woman.

First meeting with professor occurs on Friday afternoon at 5:00 pm. Since he has an important task at that day, they don't meet on campus, but at consulting office owned by her mentor.

Good afternoon professor, she greets on a man over sixty years old.

What is your name? What is your intent and purpose?

She smiles and nods a head as a sign of respect for a professor.

My name is Ellysabet, I am called Elly, a student who will prepare a final project.

Oh you are Elly, take a seat please my son, professor replies.

She afterwards gives a letter of introduction from her department and outline of task. Professor welcomes her plan, however, he writes notes on a sheet of outline agreed.

She now races against time. Work must be prompt and completed six months ahead. The plan is likely fulfilled. In addition, she is a clever woman, data and reading source are enough. What is needed now is information processing skill. She determines to produce good work. For that purpose, she visits television station to collect extra data still needed. Her visit is welcomed by television station called National Television. It is owned by successful entrepreneur who handles print media.

On the second visit to television office, a company leader, she is a forty years old woman, pays attention to Elly. She used to be called Mrs. Cartin, holds a broadcasting manager. The figure of student named Elly has known the time ago through news aired by television stations. She includes the best in a writing competition. The company where Cartin works aims to increase its servant to the viewers. With the plan, they intend to increase the number of employees. Elly is digging information on that office, then her personal data is recorded in the personnel department. After lunch, Mrs. Cartin calls Elly by phone.

Good afternoon Elly, I am Mrs. Cartin of national television, how are you?

I am fine, may I help you?

Cartin tells recruitment in the company. She further encourages Elly to send at once a job application. The plan, new employees will start work next four months. She doesn't waste the time. Two days later she sends letter of application complete with required number of supporting data.

A month before completion of thesis, she gets call letter. The letter said that applicants will soon undergo psycho test. She lives it well and is declared eligible for second stage of the test. At this stage, each participant is required to answer questions on work of news collector, scheme is written test. Exam lasts for two hours. At this stage, the remaining participants are 95 people of the original 150 participants. Received information after the test is finished saying that, the exam results will be announced by postal mail. The announcement is scheduled for next month. For participants who passed will continue with interview.

Elly is hardworking woman. So, she doesn't want to bother thinking the exam results she went through. Before announcement comes, she busies herself with paperwork nearing completion. This work makes her forget that clock is moving. She realizes having spent a month since following the second test after receiving letter from post office clerk. It is announcement letter of second stage test. The content is to ask her to come next week for an interview. She comes on the appointed day. Interview needs twenty minutes. Decision is produced by unanimous way, she passed.

The phase of the test continues. Reporting duty of journalist should be supported by excellent body condition. So, passed participants are asked to take a cover letter to hospital, they are asked to follow the medical test. She is one of prospective employee wants to attend the medical test. Needed employees are five people.

Five candidates have received the result of the medical examination. Four candidates including Elly were expressed health while one another failed. Based on the test by the doctor, failed participant was suffering from high blood pressure. It means that participants eligible become new employees of company are four people. They work at beginning of a month. An exception is made for her, it can be run because she soon will take the final exam. The company wishes her to work after an exam.

Final exam takes place on Saturday starting in the morning to finish. On appointed Saturday, she comes in time with two of colleagues undergoes the same test. She wears light blue shirt combined with a dark blue skirt, holds a book with a blue cover that is her writing. Her eyes radiate cheerful mood while her performance looks relaxed. It maybe a picture of readiness for an exam in just minutes to begin.

She gets first turn of three participants, time shows at 9:30 am. She walks into exam room. Five lecturers have waited for her, they will test her ability. First she does percentage of content of work then continues with question and answer event.

She spends an hour then walks out. Her steps show she has no problem in answering questions. Friends then shake her as a sign of moral support, she joins the crowd of friends. Now is the time for following student undergoing final exam.

She and friends are loyal to wait until the three participants finish performing their duty. After midday, a lecturer asks them back into room. Now is thrilling moment, the test result is soon reported. Team comprises five people. The man who acts representative is most senior professor, he is her counselor. Professor speaks, students are happy. They graduated with excellent honor. Attendees shake their hands as a sign of congratulation.

The day is a happy day for her family; she returns to house. Mother and siblings have been waiting for her at front door. They greet her with a sense of joy and tears of a mother; they embrace. Congratulation my son, mom says while weeping with emotion

The happy time they experience continues with dinner at a restaurant. Her father was dead, so, someone acts as head of the family is a mother. There are places to eat, they choose a restaurant near the home. They are happy, at least, Elly in next few months will assume responsibility, helping mother and siblings.

She starts new life, today is the first day she enters the office. She meets friends, chatting for a moment and then facing a boss. That day she doesn't have tasks, she is asked to read a fraction of news having been broadcast. Such job she lives for a week. Second week is learning to turn information ready to be read in front of glass screen.

A month after doing the duty, she gets a right. The salary she receives is enough to meet simple life. Most salary is transferred through teller machine into mother's account. After pressing the transfer button, she phones mother in village she sent money.

Oh my Lord, You are Great, mother says. My son, you have a good accomplishment; you are never arrogant and should always remember God. It is intended she doesn't fall into heresy.

Elly's career shows bright spot after she has worked for six months. Company's policy appoints her to follow outside training which aims to strengthen capacity. Training lasts for a month, cost of training is covered by company. During training is running, company frees her not to enter the office. But when she has a time, she visits the office, just to stay in touch with co-workers. She doesn't waste the opportunity because she realizes that it opens opportunities to achieve more brilliant career. No day without learning as she does during a whole month. End of the training period is characterized by a certificate stating someone has undergone training in political science. There are words on the certificate that says satisfying achievement.

The more opportunity comes, she is assigned to cover socio-political and economic news. Over her duty, she often interviews political figures. News she gains further are packed into interesting broadcast in electronic media.

Many ups and downs she experienced on the field she elaborated over the past three months. One of them was meeting important officials. Otherwise, she often got terror of person or party disliking the news she covered. The most frightening was goal to finish her. Those were delivered by text message.

In particular predawn, the phone is ringing. She wonders why someone calls her at that moment. She picks up the phone, a caller is an official minion. He asks to stop the story to an official consuming illegal drug. She argues, covering the news is the journalist duty. The threat is ignored; the show continues. He threatens to hurt her.

The afternoon before sunset, she goes to specific location intending to interview an official with a state. She, with two employees, are escorted by company driver. On the way, they drive a car fast. An outdated car follows them. They are approached, and the car is hit; it causes damaged, but passengers survive. Quarrel occurs, the driver is yelled, and she is scolded. The debate continues, police comes and asks them to the office. The issue is resolved, crashing party is expressed awry. A sentence is not body cage, but guilty party must pay cost of repairing the car.

Frightening terror passed a few days ago, a new terror happens. It is horrible enough. Bandit style men come to see her the minutes she got home. Neighbors know they had waited for hours before she went home. With bulging eyes, they shout her and they finish her if their wish is refused. She asks their objection. Don't load the corruption case committed by head of particular place, such is their answer. After delivering the threat, they leave her house. They express an anger when turning motorcycle.

Journalist organization has a code of conduct. During doing journalist work, she still obeys to ethics. The threat she received was a risk the work of a journalist.

Next threat happens. Two spooky-faced men are back waiting for her around the house. The younger brother suspects gestures of the two men. He then sends a message and advises her to postpone a return to home. Advice was admitted, she has arrived at home just before midnight after suspected people left their house.

She is never quiet, terror is timeless, it could come any time. A week later she gets harder threat. Her life will be snuffed out soon. This threat causes her flee to boardinghouse near the office. The new occupancy brings calmness, at least an uninvited guests don't meet her. She returns to home when getting an information explaining safe. The threat subsides after displacing for two months.

She the days felt to live without terror, a strange letter is sent to her house. Who sent is unclear. After being read, phrase in it makes her suspicious, she was invited to come to interview state officer. Invitation was weird because it was delivered by someone who claims to referred officer aide. She thinks, such legislation never come to reporter. It

may be a trap, she ignores.

One trap passed, other trap comes, the modus is different. She gets job offer at a company with good salary. Bid was sent by postal mail. She was asked to prepare job application and was delivered by herself. Job offer was strange and suspicious. This case should be made clearer. A younger brother helps to find the office. It is unnoticed and locates in a populated place.

She is bored to get terror threat. Her ugly experience is shared with work colleagues. They argue, if threat happens again, it should be reported to police. Advice is done when new threat comes, she reports to police. Since then, police often guards her. She is unhappy, no freedom.

Throughout this year, organization of journalist noted violence experienced by journalists. The statistics showed number of fifty cases. A concern was experienced by print journalist. Dead rat was thrown at his house by unknown man. As a result, his father shocked and died. This was possible because of the drug issue involving people.

Issue of terror she experiences is serious enough. Corporate leader doesn't want terrorism and violence as above experienced by her. Wise behavior is taken, she is planned to move part handling an overseas coverage. Company prepares mutation letter. New assignment makes her frequent travel to abroad.

The first place she visits is lion country, Singapore. In that country she uncovers news related officials keeping money in banks. Published news has corrupted large enough money, it could support a family of up to seven generations.

She moves from one country to another country. This time she visits a country in Asia engaging in war. When she is on scene of war, bullets whistle sounds. She often lies in desert due to onslaught conducted by one of warring party. It is not only that; she suffers minor injury as result of splashing of objects beaten by stray bullet.

People know looking for news sources at the conflict zone is dangerous task. She experiences such event when serving in the African continent. Two countries where the population is black men are having a border dispute. Her body with white skin and straight hair attracts the warring party. A soldier yells at her. Interrogation happens, and she is locked up in a secret room. The question leads to someone as suspected spy. After being yelled then abused and her face is spat. The culprit has never brushed teeth for a week, so his saliva smells pungent. She is moved into another room. It is tense time. A soldier no longer considers her as a prisoner, but it leads to woman harassment. The soldier looks at her from head to toe. She is scared to watch him fascinated to see her. His breathing is struggling as sign of lust controls his mind. When he will conduct the rape, his boss comes and witnesses his immoral action. Then the soldier stays in underwear. The Boss asks him out, and he is put in military prison. Local rule says, he has violated military ethic, because he has harassed a woman, he wanted to rape. The news says he is found guilty and dismissed from military membership. An interrogation against her continues, identity card is checked, and other letters stating that she is television journalist. She is released when investigation is finished. Experience makes her to be repatriated to the homeland.

Eleven

Terror in the country is safe after she underwent foreign affair for six months. May it happen again? No one can answer. She prays to God to be kept away from various threats.

Atmosphere is still safe after the days she sits foot in the office. She returns home the hours after sunset. A strange case happens. She is amazed at crowd of people around her house, three police officers secure the scene.. What is happening? There is traffic accident. Since it, a woman suffers minor injuries while the man who was driving motorcycle died.

That is true, the world is a theater which has various dramas. But whatever we do produces a result. It will result a happiness if we do a goodwill. Otherwise, the result is bitter if we do a poor deed. Traffic accident is a picture of earlier opinion. Dramas played by victim was terrorizing to her, then the result will be bitter, he died of traffic crash. May his soul be received by God.

Her work becomes a people attention. She met fugitive of convicted of corruption cases. The results of an interview are broadcast on television complete with pictures. Where did the interview take place? It is still a question mark, but suspicion happened in the country. The days after airing, she is called by police as a witness. she doesn't violate an existing law, police calls were ignored twice. She argues the reason should be kept secret. The third call was then received. It underlines, she will be called by force if she rejects the call. The journalist work belongs to institution. The company intervenes, and the case is handled by law department. She is still not willing to come. Police faces legal manager of company. This case is to the people attention related to law enforcement. There are siding people, others reject. Repellent is university academic, they are much more than receiver. Rule says, the source of information should be kept secret, because of part of ethics code of journalistic.

This case makes her famous, the news gets to village of birth. Her mother worries daughter will receive disaster caused by the problem. Reality is different. After the matter is completed, she gets job offers in electronic media. She has felt at home in current company, bids are rejected.

Her performance receives an award from the company, rank is now as a supervisor. Her career is so fast as meteor motion in sky. Terror has passed, new challenge arises. Her performance makes friends jealousy. A case produces unpleasant result, she is rumored as

businessman's mistress. Others have said she often has a sex with several people leaders and officials. Workers are wise, they can judge who is right and wrong. Gossip on her lost in time, no one employee at company believes the gossip. Even one of the leader issues a circular calling on employees of the company for no more parties issue news irresponsible. The circular yields good result, working atmosphere becomes more conducive.

Life doesn't go well. Sometimes it passes the hollow road, at other time it can find sharp gravel. Amid rising achievement, she gets ugly news, her mother suffers an ill. Father has died, so mother care costs become part of her load. A lucky comes, health can be restored by a doctor. But her savings was divided to pay for treatment. She is a noble son, devotion to the mother is conducted with sincere. She argues, anyone can seek money. If mother died, no way make her breathe.

She is a rising star winning the trust. Within the next days she will be assigned to the United States to undergo a training. Plan is heard by boyfriend, Wolter. Before she goes to overseas, he meets her at home. He comes in the evening, sits in front of her and smiles at her sweet face. Gaze makes her fascinates. Warmth and hope makes her want to be with him. She says, don't you understand my heart? Please tell me our friendship over the years. I have to be candid; Sadness and sorrow befall me, and I am stepping on the gravel love. You repay and direct my love. My love has sure aim so it works as foundation when the storm shakes life. Her statement is answered. Elly, once again I remind you that human being can only try, but God dispose mate. We pair or not, God knows. I hope you understand and realize what I have just said. A man you wish is your best choice. You will no longer go to America, you succeed at what you do.

He hands her a letter in sealed envelope. Does it contain love affair? She asks. He laughs. The content are privileged and confidential message. She asks the special purpose as he says. I am ready to explain the privilege of this letter, but you must follow the needs I ask. She replies, well, I will take part at your command. And, he explains the letter has the answer to her questions related to their love. She can read it when getting a permission. She agrees and receives it. They split up the minutes later.

She is now in America for ten days training, the remaining time in four days later. She is bowed sluggish after the seconds to access the Internet. Her breathing falters and her heart is pounding. A condolence comes when opening an email account. Who sent news is Jordan, he is Wolter's best friend at the university. Message sent by electronic mail tells her that Wolter has died. His body was buried at the birthplace. She is crying. Her hope to make Wolter as husband vanished. God has another plan, he has passed forever. She doesn't suspect her boyfriend left her. His health looks fresh at last time they met.

After undergoing training, she buys souvenirs, key chains and pieces of T-shirts, those for close friends. She buys ticket and leaves the superpower country. A trip to homeland spends twenty hours. Cool atmosphere inside the plane makes her fall asleep during the trip. She arrives in the country in the morning before noon. A meter taxi takes her to go home.

On descending from the taxi she is greeted by her younger brother. He tells her that Wolter has died. Oke, I have got information; she says. It is time to open special letter she received the days ago; she opens an envelope, her eyesight is directed to it.

Dear my beloved, Elly

Elly is my hope, you are dearest woman; you differ from thousands of women I knew. You are a heroine; I have never had poor purposes toward you, let alone mean to hurt your feeling. I want to be with you until the end of life.

My heart and mind rejected love when I was studying in Europe. I tell you, I never hate you, I don't have a new girlfriend, and my parents were enthusiastic to you. They expected you to be a daughter in-law. But their wish should be thrown away.

When I was in Europe, my health was compromised, then I went to hospital for treatment. Laboratory examination result proved that I was suffering from kidney disorder that was known from the results of my blood sample. Further information said that anyone suffering from this disease will not live long. If we get married, so maybe you have become widow in young age.

I don't know when the death picks up me. But the days ago, my health was getting worse. I predicted my end was getting close the days before I met you. Then, I went to the hospital. And doctors argued, my illness was acute, they cannot handle. It encourages me deliver the letter to you. I think your questions have been answered. And I don't want you wait for uncertain answer, I won't bury my love to you, but please forgive me if I didn't want to be honest with you.

As smart woman with noble minded and nice genre, I am sure men are interested in you. Get on your ambition to build harmonious family. So search for your match today. I suggest you not to forget to pray to God during search for a mate.

Failure in love doesn't mean everything is useless. Failure must be resolved. Happy days passed, start with new love. Live your life and never tired of addressing the issue. Thus this letter I command to you, I love you till the death picks up me, thank you.

Signed

Wolter

She is crying sob; she doesn't think a poor luck for him. That day she has returned from America, her body is still tired and she doesn't visit the office. She sits on chair in the corner of room, is sad for the interesting moments with him the time ago. It has gone, the remaining is fond memory, hard to forget but pain to remember.

He has gone, but it doesn't mean she forgets his kindness. The late afternoon, she with Jordan and Ryna visit the prospective in-laws. His parents are at home. Her presence is greeted with tears. They hug each other as sign of deep grief. She then says I condole. Please sit my son, mother replies while pulling up a chair for Elly. Because they are sad, their talk stutters. Tears flow when considering the wonderful memories with him. The talk is closed with prayer led by father.

Live in capital runs for twenty-four hours, any time is bustling with duty. That night she is lonely. After leaving the prospective in-laws, she goes straight into the bedroom but she is brooding. Her mind is far into space and it stops at nice memory when she was in high school. She left her lover having the same nature with Wolter; she is sad. Two men ever loving her had gone forever. Now she herself is alone, living an uncertain life.

The next day in the morning, she is heavy to step into the office. But as wise woman, she puts a duty, arrives at office on time. Friends greets her presence with warmest regard. They say congratulation on her success. She enters room and works. Duties have piled, she works in time.

Twelve

She is junior employee, but the workload has been solid exceeding other employees with her contemporary. It thanks to her proud achievement. Now she gets an extra workload, It needs special skill to do. That is the reason the company sends her to America.

She returned from America a year ago; the company plans to send her back to that wealthy country. She bears to interview well-known businessman engaging in information; he is Bob Gate.

He is a busy entrepreneur, anyone needs necessary preparation to meet him. An appoinment should be prepared two weeks before the goal runs. To impose the goal, a preliminary information is needed, and gathered by the Internet. Public relation does it.

Early information is enough, the next stage is a negotiation. A small team composed of three staff is sent, this includes Elly and Johnson. The team is led by Public Relation Manager; she is 32-year-old-woman, Ratna. They set off on given day using government-owned airline. They arrive in New York, USA, in the early evening, stay at five-star hotel and rest until morning.

New York City atmosphere where Bob Gate lives is dense and crowded. The temperature is cool. Humans are busy doing daily work. In this city, they begin the task; they contact the public relation of the company. The company they will visit was called Micro Computer International. The people know it well; it locates in the city center. They are easy to reach it because near to the hotel where they stay. The traffic is regular, so no traffic jam in the city, it eases their journey. Good morning Sir, Ratna says to security official. She explains the purpose of their visit. The security officer directs they meet the public relation of the company. This field is led by Ms. Tina, she is blonde woman with ideal tall. She receives them at the meeting room equipped with space heater. One by one team member led by Ratna introduces their self. They state a purpose; they find no problem, everything goes as applicable procedure. The conversation spends an hour and half, problems are unresolved, the remaining parts are only the form of administrative needs. Ms. Tina has another agenda, so Ratna and friends should end the meeting before the mentioned time. Agenda is charged in the morning. So, they are scheduled comes back in the afternoon at 15:00 pm.

Time at the moment shows 12.00 at noon, their stomach is hungry. They go to the nearest restaurant serving healthy and nutritious food. Visitors are from Asia, others are American population. Ratna, Johnson and Elly order the same menu, grilled chicken and lettuce as vegetable. Stomach rumbles, it causes served food taste delicious. Bill is paid by credit card, Ratna signs it. A moment later they leave restaurant and return to hotel.

Professional workers uphold discipline in managing time. As professional employee, Ratna upholds agreed schedule. She and friends have set foot in the office fifteen minutes before 15:00 pm. They sit on chairs available waiting for notice.

Good afternoon Mrs. Ratna, public relation staff, Ms. Maria, comes to see them. She motions so they meet with Ms. Tina. They walk to her den. She asks them to complete and sign documents consisting ten sheets. On this occasion, Ratna asks questions to information that have not been answered. They discuss important topics such as the time during the interview and people can enter the room. They find no problem; the meeting is closed while enjoying snacks. The final agreement sets the day of interview. As an agreed, schedule of interview is conducted in the morning in the next two weeks.

The atmosphere is getting dark. They don't go straight back to the hotel, but they move toward the entertainment center. Place they visit is simple cafe providing music room. They are laid in place until midnight.

Ratna, Johnson, and Elly are now in homeland. Besides doing a routine works, Elly prepares the task related to the interview. To add her insight in interviewing a key person, she discusses with senior having position as broadcast manager. He gives her opinions important to be asked. Other important questions she has to ask are those related to the company's business development.

The remaining time stays the days longer, so she often leaves work toward at 21:00 pm. After 17:00 pm, they are still busy at work to prepare for an interview. The work they do among others is playing back recorded interviews. Officers are directed where the right position for photographer when taking a picture.

Now is Friday on April, the interview is scheduled to take place on 25 April. Elly and friends plan to arrive in New York two days before the day of interview. They avoid fatigue,

a smooth plan is arranged. So, one day is used to break, while the remaining one is used for special discussion. Besides Mrs. Ratna who serves as the public relation manager, in their group records a man, Rudy, his position is broadcasting manager.

They gather in the office and are escorted to the International Airport by brown car-owned company. At the airport they are short break while enjoying light refreshment. The remaining time can only enjoy a bottle of soft drink. They set off at 13.15 pm using plane produced in Germany.

A moment after the plane carrying them landed at the airport, Ratna contacts the hotel where they have stayed. The hotel rooms are empty, they are straight from the airport to the hotel named New York Hotel. It has complete equipment for occupancy by reporter. What they are doing now is short break. They are relaxed, each one is sitting in chair while enjoying television show.

The meeting led by Mrs. Ratna takes place in the morning. Atmosphere of the meeting is filled with questions and answers related to the plan. The first session lasts until 12:00, then they enjoy lunch, it ends at 13:00 pm. Work plan has not finished to discuss, so the discussion is reopened at 13:30 pm and finished at 15:20 pm.

They are not going anywhere at afternoon except chatting on the hotel veranda. It differs from what Elly does. She enters hotel room, turns on the television and she is busy pressing the remote button. Her hand stops pressing after finding television shows as her will. Because of curiosity of interview in which the next day she will do, she then selects news broadcast. It is interesting and related to her job as television reporter. She enjoys the entire broadcast news. The nightfall comes, she turns of it. The bath fittings such as towel, soap and toothbrushes are available, she steps into the shower and washes a whole body.

She comes out of the hotel room wearing jean trousers and dark red T-shirts. She doesn't forget to wear a jacket to protect body from cool air. A brown hat covers her straight hair. A clothes she is wearing are well with her condition. She gathers with friends because they promise to eat dinner together, then they go to the nearest cinema for watching.

New York city temperature in evening is cool enough for someone living in tropical country. This becomes consideration for the National Television group of employees whether they will visit another place or staying at the hotel. They cannot stand facing the cool air, they choose go straight back to the hotel. Another important reason is obligating performing task of an interview.

The morning weather is sunny, the air temperature is cool, but they are ready to run the task. With the help of the hotel concierge, two taxies are called to transport them to the office. The fee is paid in cash as soon as they arrive.

Local security officers have been told that their company will be visited by guests. Ratna and colleagues are known from uniform they use, white shirt with striped blue. Written on the uniform is corporate identity, National Television.

They are asked to be ready, the interview will begin. Bob Gate has been waiting in the interview room. Within seconds, the group of Mrs. Ratna is allowed through, Elly sits across from Bob Gate, the interview begins. It is broadcast into homeland, watched by million viewers including Elly's families in village. Mother is delighted when the daughter comes up on screen. Interview makes her name shining in village, brighter than the light of moon at night.

Other villagers are happy to see her appear on the screen. Her achievement causes they change her name into the Star of Village because she is the only one villager to reach the encouraging achievement. People in the village are happy today. This differs from what is perceived in New York where she is conducting interview. The live broadcast is the first time she does, she is experiencing tenser. But, during the interview takes place, the tension remains under control.

The interview lasts for a full hour, break occurs when the advertisement is served. Breaking times are used for drinking hot tea on the table near her seat. Once the interview is complete, Bob Gate is asked to take pictures. He doesn't mind; he stands at the middle flanked by Elly and Ratna. Other journalists help to perpetuate the interesting event.

The job in New York has been completed. Now they take a time souvenirs to nearest shopping center. They buy items that will be presented to the family and close relatives. This job is tiring, but memorable. They return to the homeland by using the latest plane produced of an aircraft factory in the United States.

They arrive in the country on Sunday. That day employees working on the National Television station are on vacation. They come to the airport to welcome her. After the plane landed, she walks toward the exit. The seconds later, friends who are waiting greet her with congratulation. They shake a hand, hug and kiss the left and right cheek.

Interview that took her to America was a long and tiring journey. Her younger brother is present at the airport. Both go home using an airport taxi. Their talk centers at a work on interviewing Bob Gate including in the top ten of richest people in America. At home, they have nothing to tell. She is tired; she enters the room and sleeps. She wakes up late in the morning, a clock hanging on the wall has showed at 9:00 am. That day she doesn't visit the office. Because fall asleep, she doesn't hear an incoming call to cell phone. On-screen has the missed calls. She presses a key; the phone is connected. She contacts her mother.

Good morning Mom, did you have questions?

Oh no honey, I missed with you.

I woke up late, so I didn't hear of any incoming call.

I wanted to know your story during in America. When do you go back to village?

I will take a leave.

Later, leave petition she proposed be granted by the company. She gets a leave. The time off is used to visit parents in village. Her presence in village is greeted by the neighbors. Her house as beeing attended by a famous movie star. Villagers flock to the house, they want to come face-to-face and they talk her job in the capital. It is not to forget, a village official is present to expresses congratulation on achievement she achieved. An officer asks the sentence. Elly, the people here are now calling your name a Star. Their reason is your grade is as high as the star, so you deserve to be called the Star of Village. Ha, ha, ha, Elly laughs out, mother smiles at the praise directed at daughter

He only spent minutes in the house, he delivers a small box. She asks the content. He answers, it has a wonderful message for you. If you are curious, please open it now. She is curious, and she opens. It has red rose flower, a flower as a symbol of love. You don't have a soul mate, so the rose signals to you so you mate soon. She laughs, but a moment later she is sad to remember her lover who has died. Mother understands daughter's sorrow, pats Elly's shoulder. Mother says, what happened was a history, let open new chapter of life. She nods and chats again with neighbors.

As sign of emotion and gratitude greeting to the Creator of the universe, Elly's family invites neighbors to attend dinner together. The event is held in the evening at 19:00 pm. Invited people are thirty families. To enliven the atmosphere, the event is fitted with entertainment such as light music echoed by local singers. Other duty she undertakes with family is a pilgrimage to the father tomb. She ponders for a moment in front of the tomb, her eyes are wet as a sadness expression. She thinks back to those wonderful moments with father. Mother is more serious behavior, she is sobbing. Both her younger brother stun silence watching mother in grief. Their visit to the tomb ends with prayer offered by Elly. God is Great.

The holiday leaves several days; she takes the family for a tour. They choose destination suitable for family that is the beach. Besides watching tourist attraction, they can enjoy a myriad of joy. They could do playing, hanging out with family, eating together or enjoying the beach waves that are chases. She controls the steering wheel of car with a payload capacity of five people. They set off through the freeway, no traffic jams on the way. The journey takes half an hour to the destination. They stay in a simple hotel with affordable charge while around the hotel grows ornamental trees presenting natural coolness. The view is awesome. Visitors spend the time by using speedboat, others enjoy surfing following the flow of the waves and others are swimming. Most of the local tourists visiting the coast are seen enjoying seafood. There are eating crab oysters, grilled fish and other seafood.

One feels incomplete if visit the beach but he doesn't swim. Blue water encourages beach visitors to throw themselves into water. In its place is available of bath location. A resident comes over them, he offers a surfboard useful as swimming tool. She is reminded of childhood days the years ago when she liked to play in water at time. Swim instinct arises, surfboard is rented. Helped by surfboard, she dabbles into water and swims. Her younger brother takes the camera and immortalizes sister's action on the beach.

Beach recreation performed by Elly's family lasts until the sun is upright above the earth's surface, it burns the skin. They stop beach event when the stomach is hungry. So, they head for the restaurant which provides beach food, enjoy grilled fish mixed with soy sauce. They leave the hotel before 13:00 pm and return to village.

Thirteen

Today is the first day she enters the work since taking a leave of absence. For a time, she doesn't do reporting duty; she handles most of the administrative office related to news. An office employee comes to meet her, brings a bundle of files and gives them to her. She has to finish on time; work is a pile of earlier duty.

Toward the lunch break, a company's staff, Eva, comes to see her. A sealed letter is handed. Please read sweet woman, Eva says as she returns to her seat. Elly smiles when learning inside the letter. The company trusts her to be a supervisor at the broadcasting department.

Lunchtime arrives, employees move from the workspace. They rush toward the food stall, others meet her to tell congratulation on the trust. She, with two friends, then walks to the cafeteria to enjoy lunch.

Employees work eight hours a day. Over that time, an employee is entitled to overtime pay. Her workload at the day is solid, so she includes the employee who does overtime job. This causes, she, during the week, has to leave the office ahead at 21.00 pm.

At second week, she work in a tourist place. In this city takes place an international meeting to discuss the oil issue. Entrepreneurs engaged in the oil industry will come there. Other participants are the officials from various countries.

She is astute, she may interview the oil leader of World Petroleum Organization. An opportunity is opened to meet and interview a developed country finance minister invited to the meeting. Her accomplishment continues. The next day, she may interview a director of world financial organization. She is proud of doing this work.

Interview produces red thread. Officials say, oil revenue cannot lift the life of people, because the result is focused on several people, in this case, they are the oil executives. The countries have great oil resources, but their people stay poor. The main reason is that corruption occurs on a large-scale. It is ironic; the state has a rich oil, but surrounding population is poor. Where does the sale of oil flow? This becomes a serious concern of anti-corruption organizations.

The head of the National Television later agrees to broadcast major news on corruption in the petroleum institution. There are important and correct data. The figures discuss the case on the mass media. Officials were suspected of corruption. People are uproar and they demand that involved officials should be found out and resolved.

That demand causes a negative reaction from the public officials marked involved in corruption. Various methods are used to keep them away from the law. They do terror and blame the media. Even more tragic, suspected official reports mass media and journalist linking with the corruption case to the police station, because unpleasant. A reported mass media is the National Television and its journalist, Elly. The issue goes to court. She doesn't throw in jail because the evidence shown in court is weak. She is acquitted of charges. The opposite occurs. The members of the civil society incorporated in Anti-Corruption society, report the official to the police. Investigation runs and ends in court. The trial goes well and the evidences are correct. Witnesses speak in the court. The trial running in the district court takes the unanimous decision. An official is declared legally and convincingly proven to have violated the law. He is given a body confinement for fifteen years. He is bowed sluggish to hear the verdict.

Today is Sunday, a holiday for office employees. The dew in the early morning is still clinging to the leaves. The sun doesn't shine yet because morning cloud still covers it. On the edge of the major road is a green field, people call it Green Place. At surrounding grows green grass, and it has been visited by people. Visitors are young people loving to exercise.

A woman in her twenties walks around it. She wears red spark training with white shirt blue stripe. A dark blue hat covers her head. Her style then resembles an athlete of Olympic torchbearer. A male visitor is watching her from a distance. He doesn't want to lose the trail, so he watches the motion of the woman's step. The man wants to tell corruption case, it should be a brief delay.

A man gets closer. Then, a white woman stops relaxing walk. She sits on the bench while enjoying a bottle of tea belonging to small traders. He recognizes her. And, good morning sweet woman, you look to be relaxed? The woman turns her face. He looks on her face; he is sure a woman is Elly. The man introduces himself named Wendy. He tells corruption case he knows. He says, the corruption case occurs in an institution engaged in education. She doesn't agreed to load it in television news, but promises to contact him on time. He leaves the cell phone number. She with friends discuss the case in the office. They agree to call Wendy for an interview at the office. She reminds him so not to forget to bring the evidences available.

A promised day falls on Wednesday at 16:30 pm, Wendy comes thirty minutes before the event starts. Equipment useful for the interview is prepared. He sits in front of the camera, faces her acting as the interviewer.

An interview ran well, lasted for thirty minutes. The result was recorded in data storage, it will be broadcast on the special show. An editorial board meeting agrees that recording is worth aired on a special broadcast on Sunday night at 21:00 pm. They agree the event is entitled "Educator Becomes Corrupter". Star button is pressed, the show broadcasts at the specified time.

As usual, special event has important, exciting and latest news. People don't want to miss watching this show. An Impression has lasted for ten minutes, Elly's phone rings. The caller hopes the show is stopped. If not, he threatens to finish by force. The threat is annoying, she ignores, and the impression continues. Delivery time is for an hour, the show ends at 22:00 pm.

Educator Becomes Corrupter Event gets the spotlight from various groups. Monday becomes a concern. The problem is that someone who should work to educate young generation has committed misconduct; he was doing corruption. Print media doesn't miss, they make this problem is the headline on front page. This issue is a warm conversation. People talk it at the bus station, coffee shop, campus and schools,

In developing countries, corruption has become an officials' culture. An officer thinks corruption is commonplace. What is unusual is uncovering corruption. Who wants to uncover corruption, he is regarded as an enemy. Various methods are used by the corrupter to curb corruption cases they do. That is taking an action against him trying to open their disgrace.

Reporting of Educator Become Corrupter case began when Elly walked in the morning. Corrupters know that she is pleasant to exercise in the morning. On a holiday, a bloated man visits Green Place, nobody knows what the intent and purpose of this man. But he looks to follow the athlete's style, wearing T-shirt, shorts, and sports shoes. He stands relaxed while smoking a cigarette. That morning she is a coincidence to take part filling a sport in Green Place. She is walking, then running faster. Visitors run in groups while others kick the ball.

Nice morning turns into cloudy. The thunder's sound and a bolt of lightning decorate the morning air. Rain wets the grass growing in the field. The visitors stop exercising. Visitors leave the site, other sportsmen are still waiting for the rain to stop. Now, she shelters under the roof of the simple coffee shop. The rain causes little visitors; they are four people. A man is enjoying warm coffee. Next to him sit friends, a black woman and another woman has curly hair. They both are enjoying hot tea. Elly becomes the fourth person to take a break at the shop. The distended man with friend approach the shop, they catch her hands and drag her into the car. A driver pushes the gas pedal. The car goes fast and disappears in the pouring rain. People witnessing the incident are unnerved because no one knows the cause. They know nothing the actors and victim. They do nothing but reporting the incident to the local security officer.

This case spreads two days after the incident. Television, newspapers, and weekly magazines make this case as a headline. People speaks the police acts. Information is collected, including the characteristics of the offender and the car used.

How clever a squirrel jumps but one time he falls. Though how great someone commits a crime but his wrong can be showed. Based on information got from an electronic tool, her position is tracked in street Heart of No 1. This place is luxury housing, occupied by the rich. Police are mobilized to that place. A police officer knocks at the door. Helper comes out and asks the intent and purpose of the police comes. The question is answered by showing an assignment letter. Their purpose is checking the entire house; they want to know anyone in house. She confuses and lets the police into the house. Police experiences none difficulties. They find Elly is locked-in a dark room. Hands are tied and mouth is covered with the duct tape. Kidnapping is uncovered at that moment. The involved people are led to the police station. The case becomes an important topic of several mass media. Data and evidences are related to corruption case broadcast by television where she works, National Television.

Police moves. Data related to the case are collected, other involved are arrested. Investigation lasts for two weeks. The case is taken to court; it waits for the hammer tap of the presiding judge.

This case makes her famous. She is known as the woman combating corruption. Her picture even becomes an anticorruption icon. News relayed to her becomes attention of the international society. A World Agency presents her special award as Certificate of Anti-Corruption.

She will continue active and will not give up covering criminal cases, despite she has faced the heavy challenge. And for her courage and achievement, she is now entrusted with the bigger and heavier task. Because of this, she is promoted into higher position, assistant manager.

She was born as an honest countrywoman. Her father raised her by applying strict discipline. Mother advised that she was humble and never arrogant. Education she received forms strong-minded personality. Heavy-duty with great risk has gone. A challenging new task awaits her. The company plans to send her back to America. She

Doesn't undergo the training nor to meet with Bob Gate, but to interview key official of America. The plan is soon. If no obstacle, it will be conducted next month. Preparations run, this includes her identity. An important work is to study protocol.

No time without work, employees of National Television work together to prepare the event. The agency often visited is American Embassy. As preliminary data, the information on her identity are sent. People have known her, so her popularity makes easy to convince the American government. Her files are processed and sent to the government officials in America. Needs have been approved a week before the interview takes place. She and friends leave for America soon.

The months ago, the group of employees of National Television led by Mrs. Ratna stopped in New York city, the place of house of American major businessman, Bob Gate. This time, the city in the USA they want to visit is Washington, the city where the key official lives. Their team is only three increases than when they interviewed Bob Gate. But the leader of the group is still held by Mrs. Ratna. Preparation in Washington is different from when they were in New York. The main case lies in the protocol stringency.

Washington is the capital city of USA. The traffic is not as dense of New York city; it looks looser. No sign rain will fall at the day. Elly arrives the minutes before the interview begins. The intimate atmosphere is coloring the event watched by million viewers, Radios are taking part.

Before the interview runs out, a woman in charge of protocol comes to remind them. She utters the phrase the interview ten minutes remaining. Elly has afterwards closed the interview while reciting following limerick. If I go into the market, I buy you frangipani flower. If I go first, I wait for you at heaven. We hope, you are a long life, thank you. The poem invites laughter of the officer; she smiles.

No ocean she could not cross, no mountain she could not climb. Such expression is suitable to be awarded to her. She has received trials, challenges, and even suffering because of her job. She argues, the work of a journalist is as walking on sharp gravel, many painful experiences. Because she is used to accepting the pain, then she enjoys it as a happiness.

She now feels happy. A few days after she could interview American high official, the company gives allowance, her salary is increased. These encourage her spirit to work hard. High salary she receives is a private affair, so no one knows how much the new salary she receives today. In addition, the company helps her with a gray saloon car equipped with air-conditioner.

Fourteen

The new duty she has to do is reporting the news in the conflict zone. What happens? A widespread protest in the Latin American country. The rally is to make local security forces tighten security by raiding every foreign citizen suspicious, this includes reporters. Five people are arrested and interrogated, one of them is Elly.

A soldier arrests her after midday and she is held in an undisclosed location. An arrest happens on Wednesday when she is on road protocol in the largest city center. She intends to cover the protest by workers and students over government policy removing the fuel subsidy and raising the cost of education. When she comes to the rally location not far from the international airport, she asks friend working as a photographer takes pictures of the line of armored combat. Before taking the picture, they were allowed by the soldier to shoot. When pet-snap is done, from the distance comes loud voice that forbids their action. No photography allowed; that is the command pronounced in English as he steps closer. He wears a military uniform, holds the rank of officer and modern communication tool. They afterwards are put in the patrol car. She meets three foreigners, they will be sent to detention room. She asks whether they are journalists. A woman sitting in front of her says they are tourists, but they were suspected of being journalists. Elly's question continues, she asks the origin of their country. A soldier in the car snaps her. Shut up, don't ask! The soldier sees goods that are brought by her and friend. He seizes a cell phone and camera. They are anxiety and fear. He orders subordinate to close Elly's and other prisoners' eyes. They carry around the city. How far the path they pass, none of the prisoners can answer. The car stops after circling for half an hour. They are descended and led to detention room. Later, they are divided into a special room for interrogation. A well-dressed man meets her. His face is haunted, mustachioed, he asks discrediting questions. When the interrogation is running, a handsome man comes while smiling. This man gives the order, so she steps into the living room. He apologizes, between you and my staffs have been possible misunderstanding, he says while handing cell phone and camera confiscated. Her eyes are closed, she is restored to the earlier place. Now she frees from the threat of death.

She moves on duty from Latin America to Southeast Asia. She visits conflict zone in the state of the country. Outstanding issue says the source of conflict is social jealousy. Local people assess the central government ignoring their interests in education and economic development. She wants to visit a headquartered of the rebel organization; they were called Justice Enforcement Organization. To meet the leader, the terms and conditions are applied. She must follow rules full of twist. First, meeting forefront staff, this part is a public relation. She obeys the terms they propose. The provision runs, eyes should be closed during the trip. They leave early in the morning the hours after the sun rises in the east. Over a dozen minutes away, they are still hearing the sound of passing cars. The next environment is silent, they no longer hear the noise of car exhaust, they may have entered the forest. Car speed drops because their path is bumpy. No cars pass except scarlet Toyota she rides. The atmosphere is quiet; it shows they are in the jungle. They pause for a moment, checks are applied in the post. The examination receives none serious obstacle. One checks their identity card. At the last checkpoint, car useful as transport in the territory is stopped. She gets out and her eyes cover is opened by a woman warrior. They appreciate the guests; she is treated natural drinks such as coconut water. The throat to dries, she drinks and feels cool. She watches surrounding, a jungle that is quiet and hard to reach. No one animal emits in that place, suitable for hiding place.

Headquarter is guarded by dozens of warriors carrying AK-47. They wait for ten minutes before the leader of the organization named Richard comes. The camera is prepared; they don't sit in the chair but on top of felled tree; the interview begins. First question is the main reason underlying the struggle of the group. A question continues, she asks what the intent and purpose of their struggle. The main purpose of the interview is the next question. She asks, what they do if the struggle is successful.

The interview should run in fifteen minutes, but the plan is canceled. He gets information from his troop through the phone. Incoming information says that a group of government troops is moving toward them. We are suggested by Richard to leave the place and he runs toward the bush. An information is right, government forces come the minutes later. They drive panzer while carrying weapons. A gun battle breaks out, we move away from the conflict arena. The passengers in car survive out of the war zone.

Toward the exit of the forest, she sees a group of soldiers. The car is stopped and an existing personal identity to be checked. A soldiers leader asks whether she knows where the warriors are. She replies, no. Her car is later welcomed to leave the site.

The road is bumpy, so the car should run slower. Along the road stands the simple homes of farmers, inhabitants are empty, they prefer evacuating. They don't want to take risk because in the residential territory was often heard gunshot.

The poor road condition shows they still have long journey. Unexpected case happens, car tire deflates. This is serious trouble, she is possible in place until sunset. A case will happen, shooting will erupt because prolonged gunfight often occurs at night. They are in the forest, air is cloudy. This time is afternoon, night comes sooner. She confronts with barrage of bullets. When the driver has finished changing flat tire, gunfire hears followed by scream. Stop! The voice snaps followed by a shot, his voice is the meters from the car. From clump of bush emerges armed forces followed by five of his friends. Raise your hands and don't stir, voice snaps again with the crack of bullets. She is calm. She thinks, the death is a risk of a journalist work. I am journalist; she says short while showing identity card. A force approaches and checks out her identity. When knowing she is television journalist, he nods a head. The atmosphere changes from tense to be relaxed. The more intimate atmosphere occurs when a troop knows she often comes up on television. With friendly way, a force suggests her to leave the location. She doesn't straight away, but she persuades troops are photographed. They agree. A friend takes camera and ancillary equipment. Swarm of soldiers is standing in a row while carrying an AK-47. After taking pictures, the force commander orders us to clean up used equipment and leave the location. Car has moved, she hears sound of gunfire deafening ears. When does violence using this gun end? We hope God intervenes to finish, so people have nothing dispute and the safe and peaceful atmosphere will be created. Their journey continues and they reach the destination that is the base camp of news seekers.

One day after lunch, superior asks her. Are you still desperate to cover news in conflict zone? She answers, I have dedicated my body and soul to the journalist work. Her answer challenges. He prepares an assignment letter intending to cover the news in the middle-east region.

She is registered as reporter entering the troubled country in early June. There are several groups of armed rebellion against the ruler. She covers news under the escort of one of the rebel groups fighting to overthrow the ruling regime. While running reporting, she in constant communicates with a friend, Ramlan, in the journalists base camp. Fierce fighting occurs in the suburb, she moves closer to the conflict zone. The moments later, her communication with him is interrupted. He tries to reach her; the result is in vain. She was reported went missing since two days ago. She was abducted by a militant group involved in dispute with the government. Based on video broadcast over the Internet, she was still alive. A speaker for the captor tells, until the news release, they haven't freed her, they still need an information. In the video footage doesn't mention the party responsible for the kidnapping. People know nothing their purpose. But she was reported suspected of being minion of the ruling government.

This conflict-torn country is known as the most dangerous territory for journalist. International Press Freedom Organization listed as many as 35 journalists were dead while 28 others were kidnapped. Most kidnapped journalists have been released. Three journalists were killed, others were still missing until now. A released journalist tells he suffers humiliation every day. The kidnappers argue, reporters are in favor of specified group. He was held captive for 100 days in dark and stuffy room, treated as animal. The kidnappers call themselves the Volunteer Ready to Die. A source says, armed group stops her while traveling by car with photographer and driver. The circulating news says it happens in the suburb of the country. Then, no one can contact her. National Television party has formed special team based at the embassy to handle the release.

As long as she is taken hostage, she hears loud explosions as sound of cannon ball. The incident makes militants members come out of base and advance into battle. Officer keeping her is only one person left. When frightening gunshot is running, she is welcomed to leave the location. A confusion comes because she doesn't know the surrounding environment. She takes a cell phone and calls the Red Cross office. The call succeeds, but she doesn't know where they meet. She directs a gaze to the around location. A text contained on road marking mentions she is in front of a building at the intersection of people struggle. For the minutes of waiting, she thinks doom is near hearing bullet whistling that never stops. A white car with the logo of the Red Cross comes closer. She stops the car and climbs into it. The shots still occurs when their distance is a mile from the prison. Travelling takes 30 minutes before she arrives at the Red Cross office. The driver escorts her to the embassy the base of liberation team; she takes a rest the minutes. During detention ran, she was treated well. They first thought she wasn't journalist. After checking her identity, they will release her. Then, a leader disappears, it caused the release was delayed.

The liberation reaches the government. Official confirms the release through the television. He says Elly kidnapped in the suburb has been released; she is on flight to homeland. Television, where she works, reports the same. On that occasion is explained that she is in plane bringing her to homeland.

There is no remorse in her mind although she was taken prisoner by the warring parties. The days later, she receives an award from various parties including the television station where she works. She smiles and accepts awards.

Don't call her name Elly if she doesn't want to charge in dangerous zone, such the sentence is often spoken by friends toward her spirit in performing a duty. This time she is covering demonstration in the country involving several parties such as labor organizations, small businesses and students.

The protesters focus an action near the parliament building. By midday, the scene is overcrowded, visited by another protester from out of town. Then, they demand the government's plan to raise the price of fuel to be canceled. They argue, if the fuel is raised, then their lives will be squeezed by the higher living cost. Most protesters make the atmosphere more uncontrollable. The police issues barrage of warning as shots into the air. Protesters are panic, run into any place and try to save themselves. She follows the flow of them, climbs into parapet with intent to avoid riot. When she wants to jump, she slips and moans in pain, she cannot move. Most demonstrators try to help her. They raise her to the ambulance and rush to the hospital. The laboratory result shows she suffers from a cracked bone. No other reason, she must follow the doctor's advice. The surgery should be done; she has to stay in the hospital ward for days. A week later, she may leave the hospital to undergo outpatient.

During illness, she doesn't work. She is in exercise to move the foot at home. In the afternoon during working hour is completed, the friends visit her to comfort. Their presence make her as working in the office, they show a nice visit. She says thank you very much for the their attention.

She interviewed the world leader, various interesting news has been gathered from dangerous zone. Insults, threat of rape and murder have gone. Her latest experience happened the months ago, she has been taken hostage by militants. While she is difficult step since suffering cracked bone on the foot sole. Experiences make her name soar in journalism. She even became public figure in news broadcast.

On her accomplishments, the company gives special reward. She is promoted to be one of the important staff at print media named Capital People Daily. It is print mass media, a group of National Television. She holds to be Deputy Editor of Leading People in the company.

Fifteen

Popularity in journalism makes her get the attention and appreciation from the company. Her name becomes known by academics. Colleges ask her to be a lecturer to handle broadcasting. Three colleges expect her, her choice falls on college where she has grown up, State Leading University. The material she teaches is basic journalism. In addition, the Capital Journalist Association appoints her as a secretary. Thus, the position she occupies no longer needs her to be in the conflict zone. She has served more in the office than in the war zone filled by bullet whiz sound. Approaching the organization's birthday, they hold a day seminar. Invited participants are students following the field of journalism, law. The journalists are invited. A speaker is a young woman with million experiences, she is Elly. On that occasion, she delivers a message to the participants that journalist serving in conflict zone must have good mental. They need to know or adjust to the local culture. She tells the need to keep health and safety. To keep a health, she suggests a journalist prepares enough drugs. To keep safety, she advises a journalist wears a bulletproof vest.

At the meeting raises journalists were killed while covering the news in conflict zone. A speaker explained that journalists dead when riot happened between demonstrators and the military. The case happened in one of the Southeast Asia countries. Rules and code of conduct protect the journalists during covering the news. But shot journalists is never explored.

At question and answer session, student argues people are reluctant to work as a journalist. They are afraid of being sent to the dangerous place. She argues, journalists who should be sent to conflict zone should have experienced. She adds, a journalist work well and be ready to accept the risks that may occur including the death. So, students must be brave working as a journalist. On one side, journalist being in conflict zone is risking alive. On other side, how noble journalist's work risking a life to report important events to society. Thus, she explains to close questions put to her. Her explanation is applauded of students attending. The next question is related to life insurance for the journalist. This problem is answered by speaker mastering insurance. She finished the task at the seminar and returns to the office.

She teaches once a week on Monday morning starting at 8:30 am until finish. This duty runs in the school year of the first semester. Since she becomes a faculty member, students become tempted to continue the journalism. it's because their teachers achieve success in that field.

On Sunday after walking around the house, she is sitting on terrace enjoying a glass of tea. She opens newspaper that becomes her subscription. As usual, she first reads the headline, and then advances to the advertisements which offers a scholarship to student and lecturer wishing to increase the knowledge. Bid comes from the Australian Government. An offering declares, the Australian Government offers overseas aid program as the scholarship to 200 students interested in exploring various programs, including broadcast program. The scholarship is known as Australia Award. News published by newspaper says the Australian Government invites those students interested in becoming the new generation of leaders of the nation to cooperate with Australian building common cooperation. After passing a test, the Australian Government promotes them to learn in one of the world-class universities in Australia. Awardees are given the opportunity to experience life in Australia and to build a strong network with people and organizations in the kangaroo country. More extensive details can be found on page 'www.australia-awards.com.'

She is a young woman with high learning spirit. So, she is interested in getting this scholarship. The needs are not too complicated; they need agency's statement where she works plus transcript for several years. The organizer will conduct written test, participants must pass.

One of the written test she lives is the English language ability. She often covers the news abroad, the English language is one of the skill she has. So, she passed an English language test. Later, she undergoes test of news writing skill. The time ago, she ever became the best entries in news writing competition on television. So she passed the test with no obstacle.

Soon, she has to leave the campus where she grew. For her purpose, she prepares documents on departure, maybe it will be completed within two to five days ahead. If the documents are available, she leaves the country for Australia.

An important document is a passport, it was expired; she renews. Another important document is a house permission in abroad which was called by Visa. She is a student; she has no trouble taking care of the two documents. They are completed on time.

Her departure is a matter of days, no other important letters she needs, except ticket to destination country. She accesses the Internet, intents on finding ticket price that varies depending on the airline. She chooses Garuda Indonesia Airways. So her departure goes well, officer urges her to be at the airport an hour before departure time at 11.00 am.

The taxi she uses moves through freeway, so her journey to the airport takes 45 minutes. She has been ready at the entrance at 10:00 am; she enters. Goods she is carrying are checked by officers, checking runs well. She is now waiting for departure. The schedule for departure on time. The seconds before the plane takes off, official asks passengers to Australia to get ready to leave. She gets up from seat, walks toward the departure gate. And fifteen minutes later, passengers are busy walking to the plane that will take them to the country where the indigenous population is aboriginal people.

The plane carrying her is magnificent; equipped with an air conditioner, so passengers are cool. The minutes after leaving the airport, she sits, takes a magazine from the seat and reads it. Cool air inside the plane makes her falling asleep on the chair. She wakes up when the plane is unsteady. This is caused by variation in air density condition. Then, she enjoys soft drink provided by the airline. The minutes later, she falls asleep again.

She has a long journey, the plane she is riding approaches the destination airport. The time shows the plane will land soon. A flight attendant tells the passengers to stay calm sitting in their seats because the plane will land. A soft sound occurs, plane's wheels touch the landing site, landing runs well. She rushes out of the plane. Thirty minutes passed, they have to leave the plane. Officers who live are staffs in charge of an airline serving the passengers during the trip.

The airport is equipped with road markings useful to guide the passengers out of the airport location. She steps to follow markings to near the exit. A blonde woman, Mrs. Diana, is waiting for Elly in front of the exit gate. Diana is accompanied by a man, Ramses. Both are agency employees handling the scholarship program. Diana waves small cardboard bearing Elly' name. When Elly is standing right at the exit, she sees Diana is in action to signal her. Elly approaches.

Hi Mrs. Diana, how are you?

I am fine, welcome to the city Sydney

Thank you, I am happy to be here.

Ramses greets, good afternoon, Elly. Let's move toward the car.

They walk to the clean white color car, it will take them to the university, a place where Elly will deepen her knowledge. Intimate conversation fills their time during the trip. This familiarity causes time is running so fast and they have arrived around the campus. Diana and Ramses go with Elly up to her new house, a hostel for students from outside Sydney. This place is better known by the name International House Accommodation. It has two floors with a capacity of 400 people. On the second floor of the building provides large library equipped with the latest books. Diana then directs Elly toward the broadcasting laboratory, the instrumentations are complete enough; she is amazed.

Before going into the room where she shades during the study, she takes her bags in the car. Ramses helps remove and lift most stuff packed in it. She further is welcomed into room to rest.

She is now a student studying in reputed university in Australia. University, where she deepens knowledge, is the University of Sydney or Sydney University, Usyd. It is the oldest university in Australia, founded in Sydney in 1850. It now becomes the 3rd best top rank of universities in Australia. In 2009, the university had 47,750 registered students making it the second largest university after Monash University. Usyd has a few specialized campuses got from various organizations over the last 20 years. The main campus is found on Oxbridge field. It includes the group of eight members, group 8 Australia university that excels in term of research. Usyd's ranking and academic achievement are not in doubt. It has a unique from the main building, its shape is classical European-style building. Campus location as painted with green paint because the surrounding is planted green trees.

There is a Sandy Beach near to Usyd, its view is amazing. That is the picture of Usyd campus offering an atmosphere of campus comfortable and quiet to learn. It is often international tourists come to campus to take pictures and enjoy the art of this historical building.

City of Sydney is recognized by the world in term of quality of education because the city is safe, convenient, modern, clean. It has diverse of cultures, nice beach, entertainment equipment and various interesting sights. Study in Sydney is a dream for her.

Usyd has 16 faculties. In associated with it, the broadcasting program includes in the group Art and Social Science Faculty. In this sprawling campus, she is registered as a student taking the broadcasting management program. If she has mastered the broadcasting, she may carry out the duty of preparing a short, medium and long-term plan. The goal is to achieve the program aim, and an expected result. This skill supports the production work, the selected program, and the broadcasting time. To carry out this section, broadcasting manager first consults with marketing manager. This job supports the goal of marketing program that is revenue from advertising.

She first day steps on the famous campus on Monday morning. She wears jacket to cover part of her body because the air temperature at the moment is cool. The first place she visits is part of the administration. First, the administration staff asks her to fill out the registration form. She then completes it by attaching transcript and the last education diploma, TOEFL score and copy of passport. Those are simple, she attaches documents.

Her duty in Sydney are not different from the years ago. When studying in homeland, she joined the strata at level one. Now, her status increases to strata at level two. No day without learning. When the lecture is finished, she visits campus's library.

One day when she is cool to study in the library, a man approaches her. Sorry woman, I am disturbing you for a moment. Are you a student named Elly? A man asks as he introduces himself named Wortel. She smiles at the name the name of orange vegetable. Her smile then stops, her face wrinkles to describe someone's face sad. The word Wortel reminds her to former lover named Wolter, he has died. This time becomes an important moment for them to start their friendship.

The next day, they meet in cafeteria. She asks why he was named Wortel. He explains that his name was given by a mother who when she was pregnant likes to enjoy vegetable wortel. Vegetable is related to woman work. Mother at first expects baby was woman. But mother missed expectation. In reality, she gave birth to a man. She hopes God bless him.

Wortel and Elly have a likeness in joining the university. He was sent by the college where he worked as lecturer, continues completing the doctoral program in International Relation. His study ran a year ago, came from the same country with her. She continued Studying the weeks ago. Learning in Australia is based on scholarship from the Australia government. She takes an expert program in broadcasting management.

She is under thirty years old, she still has high learning spirit. Her work in Sydney is nothing except reading. When she has a spare time, she takes it to relax. Tenacity to study makes her be known by friends as a bookworm. She comes up as a tutor for friends for each discussion related to the course material. Her intelligence is proven when mid-semester exam results are announced.

She is a remarkable woman, her achievement was satisfied. The Announce proved she was the best student of dozens of friends taking the field study of broadcasting. Courses taken passed with the best value, A. Based on achieving the study, she is expected by education bureau of Usyd becomes outstanding lecturer. Usyd will do it when her studying has gone for a year. She doesn't refuse. She responds with simple sentence; I hope to meet your expectation.

After the semester exams passed, she stops to study for a week. Free time she uses to frolic with new friend, Wortel. Seen from the body shape, he differs compared with Wolter. He is higher and stockier. They have likenesses, but both have typical disparity. Wolter is quiet man while Wortel is humorous. The nature of humor often makes people laugh. She is interested in him.

On the last day of holiday, Wortel takes her out to the beach, she agrees. They want to enjoy the nice beach in the morning while removing the load of thinking they felt during this time. They leave early in the day using a car belonging to him. Air is cheerful, no sign rain will fall. They see the wave of roadside trees showing flowing air. They arrive at Sandy Beach in time, taking a rest in the simple shop. Their stomach is hungry, they order meal comprising potatoes, fried chicken and salad as young and fresh vegetable.

Meal is finished, they then talk the course. She tells an involvement in journalism, and lecturer at university. Later, after course is completed, she will return to homeland to continue earlier work. He asks whether she has companion of life candidate. She doesn't want to explain the good and sad time happening in the past with her boyfriend. The question is answered with the following sentence. Humans can only try, the problem mate, God disposes.

She is tired of sitting on the beach for more an hour. But she catches his movement that wants to create closer friend. He orders two bottles of soft drink, the one is given to her. Extra question is posed. Elly, when do you get married? Women want to mate. This time, she focuses on study. If you want to know when I will get married, we should continue friendship until we both return to homeland. He nods over the answer. They leave the beach at afternoon.

After the dark passed, the light comes. Monday passed, Tuesday comes, and so on until a week. The first week passed, two weeks is waiting. For executive named Elly, a day for 24 hours is short. Time passes so fast, she has been a student on campus Usyd for a year. Announcement of second semester exams was out. The result was very satisfactory; she was declared to be the best student following broadcasting program.

An achievement she reached encourages university party to offer scholarship package. Usyd will finance up to complete the doctoral program. Usyd issues term and condition, she must become a lecturer at the university that has graduated professional workers. She has a high moral responsibility, she won't disappoint the institution that brought her. Offer is rejected, she prefers serving in homeland.

Outside the lecture, she spends more time in the broadcasting lab and library. In fact she has taken square off delving the Newspaper Production for dissertation.

One day after class, a professor at the campus, Professor George Adam, meets her. He invites her to talk for a moment. How are you, Elly? He asks to begin their meeting. I am all right, Professor. The conversation continues to study the problem. Before coming to Sydney, what jobs did you do? She explains that besides being a lecturer; she handled the print media with the post of Deputy Chief Editor. He later suggests that her dissertation addresses Newspaper Production. I agree, she answers to close discussion with professor whose hair are white.

Her moment to study in the kangaroo country is no longer. Now she has entered the fourth semester. The lectures are finished, the remaining is dissertation, the need for student to achieve Master's degree in mass media. Professor Adam ever told her a message, she remembers what he said. She comes to face to his office asking him as faculty mentor into preparing the dissertation. Adam is happy to pass the wish, he is happy to guide her.

Adam has a print media company, so he masters how to produce newspaper done from upstream to downstream. Her task is lighter because besides mastering the field, he has various reading materials which can help a student as her. By studying hard, she can make the task title within four weeks. Comprehensive learning instruments supported by modern laboratory and guided by an experienced lecturer makes her thesis goes well. Toward the final task is completed, Adam calls her. The goal is to test the extent to which she has mastered the material of dissertation. The 65-year-old professor is amazed; his questions can be answered. Elly, you are the best student I have guided, thus; the sentence spoken by the professor with 175 cm of height. He welcomes her to leave the room.

A day before the exam of the dissertation, Wortel comes to the hostel where she lives. He intends to offer gratitude to the Creator for the immediate success of her dissertation examination. They gather in the living room sitting face-to-face. He bows a head and says a prayer to Almighty. On that occasion, he prays, so she gets a God's guidance. He realizes that she needs enough rest. So, he wants to spend no time. He excuses himself while pronouncing a sentence, good luck taking the final exam.

She is a brilliant student; she is often a tutor for friends. Even friends call her a teacher. When she is stepping toward the exam room, friends go with her step. Good luck Teacher, a friend comments when she sets foot right in front of the door of the exam room on the second floor of campus building. When she gets into the room measuring 7 x 8 square meter, five Professors are ready to test her ability. Their representative is her supervisor, Adam. After he introduces her, she is welcomed to explain the detail of dissertation to the testers. The time is long enough; she spends 40 minutes explaining dissertation material from beginning to end.

Now is turn to the professors in action, they ask the teacher. Each she finishes answering questions of the examiners, smile and nods of head are created bode her answers satisfactory. No question she could not be answered. As a snake preys on mice, prey was swallowed without residue. Debriefing goes more an hour, the tester Professors have no more question. Adam speaks again, he asks four other Professors whether they want to ask questions. They are silent, no sign to ask. He welcomes her to leave the exam room.

Five Professors discuss intending to assess of her ability and work. They decide and announce she passes with honor. She is now entitled to Master degree in mass media. She shakes hands with the tester professors, followed by congratulation from friends waiting around the building.

Sixteen

She has disappeared from the screen during two years, now she is in the homeland. Her big name as television reporter has not faded. When television employers know she has been in the country, job offers keep coming. She has good moral, so in choosing a company to work, consideration is not on salary and allowance provided. She is loyal to the company that raises her. Coming bids are rejected, she remains at her stance, working on present company.

As an employee holding Deputy Editor of leading people in the famous newspaper, she intends to raise the name of the print media. To run her aim, she discusses with senior, Anton; he holds Chief Editor. They agree to hold news writing competition in print media. He asks her to draft a proposal to do the program. She intends to recruit talented young writers. So, the company expresses the following provision. When registration is open, participants is at least 25 years old. Though the registration is free, her big name and experiences adds to the splendor of the registration atmosphere. When the registration is closed, thousands are take part in competition. Most of them come from the university students and fresh graduates. The committee notes two thousand two hundred and twenty-two participants to register.

The management party doesn't want this event loses its spirit. They invite experts in journalism and print media as members of the jury. Invited experts are the Leader of Capital Journalist Association, Mr. Weber, Professor of Mass Communication at State Leading University, Professor Donald Martin. Another expert is an owner and a Leader of a print media company, she is a 48-year-old woman, Tina Tulalit. Besides the three above, other jury members are hosts, Anton, and Elly. They compose of five people; the team is known as the Five One.

The team is facing the heavy challenge. Participants are over two thousand people, so they have to workday and night to check and assess manuscript received. When they are facing the important issue, they even meet until midnight.

Hard work results in good achievement. Of the thousands of participants sign up, the team decides to best five participants. The fifth best participant is achieved by a woman, Yuli, she is 22 years old, a student at the end of the university in capital. A fourth winner is a 24-year-old man, Johan. He graduated from University in a state three months ago; he is looking for work in capital. The best to three participants comes from the southern state in the country. When registration was open, he sent a manuscript through the Internet. He is Rudy, 25-year-old man with the status of private television employee. The second-best participant is won by a woman, Eva. She is an only child and just the days graduated from mass communication major of the university in capital. The best achievement is won by a man with glasses, he is broadcasting graduate from major university. His age is 24 years and now is serving an internship at the private television. The best of five participants are welcomed to prepare job application to company. Based on the company need, added employee will be required soon, they will change data into news.

Besides being enthused by the talented young generation, this event catapults the company's name. Demand increases 20 percent from normal. Added revenue from advertising rises approaching 25 percent. During the last six months, company's rank is becoming the order of best two -selling of print media in capital. Shareholders compell to reward an employee who excels. Award falls on the talented young woman, Elly. From the 1st of August, she is named the number one in editorial replacing Anton as Chief Editor. Congratulation and good luck to you.

She cultivates the press; it makes she gets special attention from the campus being. A group of students comprise four people come to see her. They suggest so media is born on their campus of useful information media as a forum for students to develop talent in journalism. The idea is brilliant; she is enthusiastic. A month later, mass media was born, it was named Campus Media. For a while, students ask her as Leader editorial.

Fly my flag, fly my Campus Media, thus cheering of students on the first day it begins the birth of media they love. Their joy continues. They argue, Campus Media will be the source of information for the students. The short-term plan, the media is published once in two weeks. If Campus Media develops better, they plan to publish it every week.

The first issue has a friction on education as the main report. Education leaders argue, in the era of the previous government, capitalization and liberalization of education didn't occur. An education expert, Professor. DR. Steven Darwin, says citizens of the relative time get an equal opportunity for good education up to university. Each clever child will be accepted at university-owned government even though he comes from a family with a weak economic backdrop. But the present government, capitalization, and liberalization of education thrives as developing the fungus in the rainy season. He tells, such education can occur because of being guided by the applicable legislation. His opinion says, this education should be abolished because more harm than good. The next opinion gets a strong reaction from the government official. The professor says, the running education shows the government tendency to wash a hand off responsibility.

Another education expert, Dr. Peter Burton, reviews the main cause of high cost of education. He argues, the rampant corruption of education funding is the major cause why the cost of education in the country to be expensive. To avoid the corruption, the accountancy must be transparent and be announced.

The headline of it makes educators voice. They hold the demonstration in front of the Ministry of Education. Their demand is that corruption in education is investigated. Anxiety comes up on any official involved in corruption cases. They are not only officials in the education department, but they have penetrated up to lecturers at university.

A lecturer, Andry, serving Dean of the Faculty of Social and Political shows cynicism toward Elly. One day she runs into him, he looks and stays away. This behavior he shows as feeling she is the most responsible person for corruption news published in the Campus Media. Since then, he feels sit on the hot chair. The rumor says he involves in corruption. He has served Dean for a year and he has a luxury house and car. Find out corruption cases in our campus. Such a sentence in poster plastered by students around the faculty.

The first issue reviewed problem of corruption, the second issue is still in the plan because the responsible party hasn't decided on major topic to be loaded.

Once on a time, a lecturer comes to meet her, he works at the college. He tells data that can be trusted. There are several educators committing immoral act, such he speaks to her at meeting held on the afternoon. On that occasion, he shows a video footage showing educators commit immorality. This information is interesting, she discusses with friends. The editorial board decides that immorality problem will be loaded as a major report on the second issue.

Agree on article of association, Campus Media publishes every Monday. The second issue arises as the decision, the headline is immorality. On the front page is written headlined, Immoral Lecturer. Here, he stays with woman at hotel. His action is shameful because he is dating a legitimate wife of a man. More news related to him is that he becomes a regular customer of the prostitute location. Added news, Campus Media carries the strange behavior of a lecturer in the sex business. News underlines what he does, and it turns out he has entertainment homes in prostitution. Their behavior is alarming. A truth of news is tested. Police explores the case, he asks people. The result is one hundred percent true. Both lecturers are discharged by the authority.

Elly's existence as chief editor at the Campus Media annoys people having moral and the law sin. Who is guilty, he tries to discredit her. They argue, she is a thorn in the flesh which if allowed to continue she may interfere with the official having violated law. So, unscrupulous men try to get rid of her from any important position, she must be removed from position of Chief

Editor of the Campus Media. Another key position in faculty is the chair of the Department of Mass Communication. In the next days, the official will leave the post, his tenure runs out soon. The guilty officials try to obstruct, so she doesn't hold the post.

State Leading University is known as a democratic campus, each post is determined by election. Friends introduce her into the candidate who will occupy the Leader of the Department. Before election day, lecturers approach another faculty so not to choose her.

Why do they fear? If she is elected, she then will take apart corruption cases at that top university. Suggestion for not to choose her doesn't run well. The election result shows she is superior to the rival. Under current rule, she must be appointed by Decree of Dean at least two weeks after the results are announced. In fact, her appointment is still waiting. A circulating rumor says delay is caused by an act of party worried over her lunge for dealing Campus Media.

Delay continues, it takes a month. When she is designated as Chairman of the Department, no academics knows. The problem is more widespread when Campus Media loads it as main news. The case becomes students attention. They gather around the campus and give speeches criticizing official which delays her appointment. A senior lecturer speaks. He is Professor of her counselor when preparing the final project the years ago, Professor Gordon. He calls for a whole range of campus to uphold justice and truth. He urges the authorities to set her. Academics respects senior Professor, DR Andry changes stance. He prepares, signs, and gives the letter of appointment to her. This decision was heard up to the corner of campus, congratulation arrives. Students don't want to miss, they come to the office to congratulate her. Today she is as top artist getting a rave review from part of campus. Once again, good luck for Elly.

Campus Media has many casualties, educators have entered to jail because of preaching. The news continues, corruption cases in the State Leading University have been showed.

What news will be published in Campus Media? The data is still being collected.

Campus Media publishes warm and interesting news, this makes people pay attention to media. Who take part are more and more, they want to present hot news on education.

Because of rapid development, at six months, she and colleagues agree that Campus Media publishes once a week. News coverage is expanded, no longer related to higher education, but including secondary and basic education.

She is busy; she wants to withdraw from top management of campus newspaper. But most students still need her energy. She is urged to keep the post as editor of leading people. The students argue, she can bridge the people interest inside and outside the campus. To strengthen management, she asks senior, Professor. Gordon, as Adviser and Protector of the media.

In the first week of the latest issue, Campus Media raises an issue on teacher shortage that occurs in vocational schools. Based on a survey conducted by an institute, vocational high school needs tens of thousands of teachers. An official at Ministry of Education says, it happens because most education graduates don't have capacity to teach in vocational school. A polytechnic graduate of diploma - 4 is more able of teaching vocational school, he adds. Because of a Polytechnic graduate is more excellent to master theory and practice than educational graduate.

Shortage of teacher hasn't received an acceptable response from public. Second Edition the next week, Campus Media publishes a warm news. The students' promiscuity comes up as headline. Rumors circulating in the society say students involve in free sex, they even plunge into prostitution. It includes an expert' opinion in psychology that says, students do free sex because they are looking for an identity. These free sex issues make ears of relevant officials red. The tail, local education officials form an investigation team to find out the truth of news. The result shows the truth, but no one party is responsible. The related parties blame Campus Media. A print journalist comes to see Elly and asks for comment related to error assigned to her. She answers, we know our officials are correct of thousand percent.

Society no longer knows she is a seasoned journalist, but it has been seeping into another issue, heroine of education observer. Over the education, an official at the ministry of education invites her to present in an Upper Middle School. She is asked to contribute an opinion on National Education Day related to adolescent behavior. She doesn't handle a teenager issue; she knows teenager lunges from books. On that occasion she describes, adolescence is a time of individual development. In addition, adolescence is a period in developing a person who lives that stretches from the end of childhood to early adulthood. A psychologist's classifies adolescence into a crucial period. An adolescence leads happy period, otherwise it leads an annoying period. She tells an important case to note. At adolescence occurs various changes, these are characterized by physical and psychological change. This change is likely to cause a particular problem for the child. If we cannot cope, it can lead to juvenile delinquency and do a criminal act. She Expresses adolescence understanding. The problems may arise including reproductive maturity needs an effort of satisfaction. And if we don't guide them by the good norms, they can lead to deviant sexual behavior. It can happen when early adolescent (11-13 years), is the best time to get to know and explore a foreign language. But, because of limited opportunity, tools and means, causing the child find difficulties to master a foreign language. Delays in language development can cause aspects of emotion, social, behavior and other personalities.

It comes up the opinion that says adolescence is a time of social thirst. It is characterized wish to hang and be accepted peer group. Rejection can lead to a sense of frustration, isolation and to make the child inferior. On contrary, a teenager be accepted peers and be an idol, he is proud and is honored. A student asks her an issue related to personality and emotional development. She argues adolescence is called time to find the identity. The quest for identity is done by 'trial and error' way. Identity crisis will lead to show unreal personality. As a result, children are depressed and moping, even making him a man having aggressive behavior. Arising results are quarrel and fight. She tells, the most important and dangerous case when adolescence is related to social behavior, morality, and religion. In line the growth of reproductive organ, comes the need to find a special friendship to another sex. If we are not proper to guide, it will result social deviant and deviant sexual behavior.

She finishes speaking before the lunch break at 12.00. Her task at that day is much, she has to attend the meeting in newspaper editorial at 14:00 pm. She leaves the meeting location after committee tells the meeting is declared finished and it will begin again at 13:00 pm.

Seventeen

Wortel still remembers when the sky above Sydney city was clean and interesting bluish. At that moment, he was cool to talk with Elly in the nice coastal while enjoying lunch and hot tea. And he remembers when he asked how longer she gets married. His wish is simple, she hasn't found her match. If expectation is true, he may create love, he thinks amid busy working as a lecturer.

Time passes so fast. He remembers their meeting when they were in Australia occurred three years ago. Today finds out her status if she has a mate. The information he got says she comes home from work around 20:00 pm. He takes the time to visit. His fate is unfortunate, as he arrives home, he gets information saying she is still meeting in the office. What time she is at home, he gets no answer. A younger brother says, when she undergoes a meeting, she will be at home at midnight. Oh, I have a time; he thinks. He excuses himself and intends to return tomorrow or the day after.

They meet two days later; it happens at the campus where she works as a lecturer. She is chatting with students to discuss glimpse of news that will be posted on Campus Media. A woman who is the administrative staff says, sorry to disturb you, Miss Elly, I found a guest; he wanted to meet you. Okay, please tell him a short wait. He is Wortel, a man she knew when studying in Usyd at Australia.

Hi, Elly, how are you?

Oh, I am fine. Have you finished your study?

I have completed it, now I am back to teach.

What is your next plan?

If the Lord blesses me, I want to get married.

She is silent wondering if he has a candidate. Then she asks.

Have you got candidate?

Wortel replies, I am looking for her.

She smiles, she understands what is meant by the last sentence he spoke. She leaves the room ordering hot coffee presented to the guest. A cup of coffee is then served by cafeteria employee after she returns.

Her work today is full, she tells him she has no time to chat. She asks whether she can help something. He expresses a purpose to put his work on Campus Media. The material of his paper is a concern to International Relation. She says, we discuss it at office. Her reason is Campus Media publishes news related to the country's education. For International Relation, your work is more precise to be loaded in the Capital People Daily newspaper. He understands and expresses an intent to meet her on next Saturday evening; she nods a head.

She is a young heroine of the nation's hope. Added information, she is a talented woman whose responsibility is a company backbone and a good homemaker candidate; he expects her. He arrives at 19:30 pm on Saturday as promised. His visit is unfortunate. When he arrives, another man chats with her. Is he a friend or close relative? He doesn't get the answer. But from his behavior, a man wants to woo her. She introduces him to Wortel, his name is Tommy. The further information explains that Tommy is young entrepreneur engaging in Production House and Event Organizer.

Wortel is an educator, he is a lecturer in university with last education of doctor degree. He is calm to face Tommy's presence. Competition for getting mate is a commonplace. He has no cynicism and no squabble, conversation goes cheerful and peaceful.

Tommy comes first, he feels having a long conversation. Nothing else he is talking, he says goodbye. He leaves Elly and Wortel on front terrace. Wortel tries to tie promise, asks her to give time for him on the following Saturday. She refuses because she wants to the village to visit the mother who was sick. He offers kindness, expresses good intent so she with him visit the village. The likeness of behavior owned by Wortel with her former lover, Wolter, makes her more hopeful at Wortel than at Tommy. She agrees with his wish and plans to go together to the village.

Wortel and Elly does the same in managing time, they are discipline. He comes in on time at 8:00 am on Saturday the first week of October. He presents using a white seamless car, a thick English book is in the backseat, he may be enjoy reading it. She gets into the car driving at normal speed. That day the traffic is quiet, car tires motion delivers them up to the front gate of the house. An old mother is sitting on the terrace, her face looks tired and her hair has been graying. The woman gave birth to Elly; she is hanging a million hopes on the daughter. Mother, Elly is missed of her affection. They hug while tears are dropping, tears of warmth, tears of compassion and tears of longing. Elly then introduces him to the mother after missed hug is completed. He smiles while shaking hands with the mother. Good day Mother, my name is Wortel, comment a man who delivers Elly to the village. Mother doesn't ask Elly who is the man. But she suspects stocky man is a daughter's choice to be life companion.

An old mother doesn't release much ado through words. Elly, your father has gone, I am old; you have worked and you are old enough, marry please, such is recommended by the mother of the eldest son. She is silent but nods as a sign of receiving advice. He blushes. Mother hopes, he can be a son-in-law.

The sun continues to move from West to East. Twilight passes night comes. They intend to leave the village after she heard mother's hope. Her mother is healthy, but she has complaining because Elly is single. He gets into the car, turns on the car engine and they go back to capital.

Mother's hope penetrates deep into Elly's mind, it pushes her to get married. Did she choose Wortel? She has no enough information to decide, she still needs more information before deciding. Alternatives are two candidates, they are Wortel or Tommy?

Wortel becomes more intensified. In the other hand Elly remains cautious, she is not haphazard to decide. She hopes, marriage is one time during a lifetime. A question comes, who is best man. She is looking for solution. Once time, she spends with Wortel. Other time, she goes for a walk with Tommy.

Wolter takes on binding her to get closer. He offers an idea inviting her to set up company engaging in book publishing. This offer attracts her attention, it doesn't take up time, and she is a woman having the interest to write. She provides no certainty, something information needs to be understood better. An outstanding issue says, he has married and has two children. She believes information is correct. For a time, she heard he received call from child. He told the following sentence. Have you eaten honey? Take a nap after eating my boy!

She doesn't want to get lost in the dead end; moreover to take woman's husband. When time comes through, She will ask on him whether he has married.

She realizes time to marry has come. But nobody wants to fail to keep the integrity of the household. Though mother's expectation should be fulfilled, she wants the marriage runs well. Any confusing information should be straightened.

The time has come; she invites him to meet at the restaurant. The goal is she wants to make sure the circulating news saying he was married. He meets an invitation, arrives at restaurant ten minutes after her. The worm in stomach is thrashing, he eats food when being served; she does the same. After chatting for a moment, she speaks in meeting core. Wortel, please forgives me if my questions are less pleasing in your heart. Tell me please! He welcomes her to say.

I got information you have married?

Oh yes, you are right; I have two children.

Where is your wife?

I don't know of her existence, but we have divorced in court four years ago!

Thank you for your explanation.

She no longer asks questions related to his marital status, the important issue has been answered. This information becomes a major consideration to continue a friendship with him.

Instead of leaving many doubts, she contacts mother in the village over the phone. She tells mother he has ever married and has two sons. As the villagers, the mother still adheres to villagers' opinion saying married to widower or widow is dishonorable deed. So, mother urges her to stay away from a guy named Wortel. Mother is hoping that she is looking for another man deserving to be her husband. Since then she keeps distance to him, she is never willing again to be invited to travel. But she still accompanies him talking on the front terrace. She keeps friendship; so it doesn't cut off soon.

He doesn't realize her decision to stay away is final. He still tries to bind closer friendship. Setting up publishing company alludes again, she refuses his wish. Her reason is busy, so she has no time to manage a new venture.

She is never willing to be invited alone, building joint venture was rejected. He assumes she has an idol man. The hope for biting in an aisle with her vanishes. He forgets the woman he knew in Australia. He sends a short sentence. Good luck Elly, may you be happy with a man you love. She cannot deny he has become her idol, sadness comes when she reads a short message. The message is answered. A human can only try, the problem mates God dispose. May God bless you and show the best way to get your life companion. Thank you for your concern over this.

How her love development with a young entrepreneur named Tommy? Does she find out love? She is not a prostitute easy to couple. As a dignified woman, she needs careful consideration to whom she should make love. She is not a materialistic woman, moral and behavior become a major consideration in choosing a mate. A man interested in her must have smallest need, an income. She thinks, the greatest wealth for a person is not real property, but invisible property such as ability and good moral. So, one can find way when finding problem in wading through this life.

Breaking a tie between Elly and Wortel reaches Tommy's ears. This makes he is more active to approach. He at least contacts her by phone. When she has time, he invites her to have lunch together. But, she doesn't throw in him, it may be the first stage of love story.

Many thousands of stars in the sky, just one is glowing fire. Thousands of beautiful women can be chosen, but Tommy sticks on Elly. Why he falls in love with her? She is an honest, noble and broad-minded woman. Besides patient, attentive, and loyal to friends. Added value she possesses is brilliant achievement. Her age doesn't reach thirty years, she was believed to hold the key position in company where she works. An advantages she owns make herself into men's idol. Tommy becomes infatuated with her. Before going to bed, he never forgets to call her. He spends most of his free time on talking over the phone.

At one time, a television station reports the famous British music group will hold a concert in capital. He contacts her with intent to invite her to witness the event. She has no other work; she approves his willingness.

When the concert takes place, he comes to pick her up to the house. He is fascinated to see her fashion. The woman of his dream wears dark blue pants and white shirt with a light blue vest. From the front view, she is as to Kate Middleton, a woman from England. While from the side view, this woman with straight-haired and white seamless looks as Hilary Clinton, a woman from America, Elly is graceful.

Be they are a pair of man and woman among thousands of spectators attending the concert. Tommy's awe of her makes his attention is more focused on her than to the music attraction. He differs from the spectators prancing with delight to music playing. Music concert finished, he is not willing to release her. The time shows at 23:00 pm; he is still trying to hold by inviting her relaxing in cafe. Today is Saturday, she doesn't mind, and she obeys his will until after midnight. They get home after watch shows at 0:30 pm.

He is optimistic to pick up her; he is more diligent to visit her. Throughout it still be granted, he meets her demand. When she wants to buy book; he accompanies her to the bookstore. Before visiting party, he takes pleasure in accompanying her to buy new shirt to shopping center. When she has spare time, he asks her to go watching a movie and enjoying a delicious meal in the restaurant. He does with pleasure because of love. He shows a truelove; she is steady with him. But as a woman, she is not aggressive to show her feeling.

On a holiday, she invites him to the village where the mother lives. She disappoints, expectation cannot be met. He gets an order to serve large corporate birthday party. As executive engaging in Event Organizer, the demand cannot be denied. Another reason is executives and officials of company will attend the event. So, this moment can add new client. But, her disappointment doesn't continue, she understands his business related to work carried. A younger brother accompanies her go to the village to meet mother giving a birth.

In the village, she explains mother on the details of a man who becomes her choice. Regard to the soul mate, she has been mature, so mother pleases to choose her own. But mother is wise, she wants to meet with man who will become son-in-law. Today is impossible, Elly promises to introduce him at once.

Both of them are busy, they don't realize they have never met for two weeks. Longing comes up on both sides, she is waiting while he is curious. He intends to call her but his phone rings; a caller is buyer, he is asked to prepare for the wedding. He is longing to meet lover, the purpose to contact her should be canceled, he goes to attend to meet a customer.

Longing is unstoppable, he tries to meet her without contacting first. She has a habit on Sunday morning, walking around the house. He estimates she is at home at 9:00 am. Estimate misses, fence, and door are closed, no resident shows a nose. He doesn't wait long and leaves the location.

The seconds after he has arrived at the house, he tries to contact her, but no one picks up the phone. Respond is sound which recommends leaving a message. At the day, he is brooding and trying to guess what happens. He thinks whether she is disappointed, cranky, and she is trying to get him away, he doesn't get the answer. Musing continues until sunset.

After dinner, he tries again to contact her, no answer. He is agitated walking to and fro; no one knows what he purposes. Maybe this one is true, he worries to lose a lover.

Air is clean in the night, it causes the moon to be in space looks bright. The clock in his room shows at 23:30 pm but his eyes have not yet shown drowsiness. Outside the house looks swarm of bats flies while eating moths flying to light. An owl sounds, he adds a loneliness. He has fallen asleep when the reverie ends with regret, regret because he could not go with her to the village.

Wall clock shows at 5:00 am, a rooster is crowing, his sound wakes Tommy from sleep. Because of lack of sleep, Tommy's body is not fresh. His memory goes to her. Could she stay away from me? That is a question in his mind.

At 08.00 am he is ready to leave for office. He takes a cell phone laying on the table in his room. He sends a text message; the answer is expected. Sound kring is heard, it signs message has been sent. A woman later speaks by phone. Good morning Tommy, I am on the way to capital. He is flowery because he will meet a lover.

Morning changed to noon, noon changed to evening and then it switched again into the morning. He tells her want to see soon; she passed his wish. Because of busy, she suggests he comes to office. So as his visit doesn't interfere the work, she hopes he comes before the lunch break.

He comes up well-dressed; he is late because of being disturbed by traffic congestion. She is the minutes of waiting; she gets up from seat while watching him is standing in front of her. They step up and get into the gray car belonging to boyfriend. In the car, she explains that she was out of town for three days. Her agenda was crowded, so she turned off the phone. Her presence outside the city is to open a representative office, it was in the city center. People in the city were well-educated, so the city was named Student City.

An issue is answered, she is not cranky and angry. The problem he faced is not because she regretted on his behavior which was not willing to escort her to the village. But her style is changed from smile becomes passive, this change is caused by overbooked workload.

They stop at a restaurant; the visitors are young executives. A visitor takes position as his wish, they take position on the left side of the building. He beams to watch her face. A moment later she asks.

What happens, Tommy? Why do you smile?

It is a longtime enough we haven't met; I miss you.

Are you still willing to go with me to village?

Oh, I am sure! I want to get introduced right to mother-in-law candidate.

She smiles to hear and enjoys favorite melon. He follows her, picks up a banana, opens the skin and swallows its fruit. He ends the meeting by drinking water in the glass. They are excused from the restaurant after meal expense paid.

The love journey is not smooth to run, it can face a great wall and carry unpleasant gossip. Ugly news overrides her. The last few days growing a gossip which says she dated with a business leader. Even the gossip grows to be unpleasant news. The gossip says she has sexual intercourse at a five-star hotel. Print media states woman's identity, her nickname is Elis. This rumor is at first spread by print media, but this changes into a major report of the weekly magazine. Televisions don't want to miss, they are busy entering this rumor at a special event.

He knows well her full name is Ellysabet, so the rumor that hits the woman with the nickname Elis makes him heavy stress. When news is inquiring, she is light to reply; the rumor is wrong. This question makes her furious, she challenges. Who says I have an affair with the employer, please show me the evidence, let me report to the police. No evidence he can show. He is silent because no mass media which includes person's name. Everything writes perpetrator's nickname. He gets a test. A party spreads a gossip at her, he must try to overcome. If he does nothing, their love will smolder.

A television reporter to clarify the entrepreneur in question, his nickname is Barry. He says, he ever met with Elly at five-star hotel, but she was in the duty devoting herself in media. He was television business leader, and she was mass media company employee, so both had work tie. At the end of the interview, he issues stance, challenging anyone responsible for the obscene news.

The rumor was without evidence, the cheating story happened to her lost in time. What remains was blowing unpleasant news. If person comes up, he will face authority.

Gossip overridden her passed, new rumor emerges, aimed at Tommy. Rumor says he has married with singer artist. Story said their love affair created the months ago. He served the client in the wedding party at the five-star hotel. A buyer expected the event was filled by a famous singer. The organizer was ready to fulfill. He contacted the female singer with nickname of Chery; they negotiated in the hotel. The rumor spread, it said their meeting continued to stay at the hotel room. Their friendship ran well, they often stayed at the hotel alone. The catastrophe came, Chery was pregnant, and she forced him to marry her soon. He could not be avoided, Chery's stomach had contained a baby. He complied with her demand; they were married.

Elly is not willing to confirm the news on him. She argues, when Chery was pregnant, then mass media published the news because Chery was a famous artist. Let time answers, such is her stance.

His way differs from what she did. She ignored, while he comes to see her clarify rumor that occurred to him. He fears, he tells the story and assures her it was a lie of a thousand percent; she nods. She says a sentence; I hope you will be the best candidate for a husband in the world. He laughs.

Eighteen

People were impressed by the story of Romeo and Juliet, amazing and fun. Tommy and Elly experience different case. Their love story reaches ears of his parents. The big challenge faces them. His father is not interested in making her as the daughter-in-law. The main reason is that she is a village woman who lacks understanding of modern human life.

Once on a time, he invites her to his house with intend introducing her to parents. At first, his father, Mr. Henry, is excited to see her showing. She is polite, respectful to parents and her career is prominent. Henry's enthusiasm toward her drops when knowing her as a village woman. Henry leaves her sitting in the living room with son, steps into a backroom while carrying a glass of coffee. His wife, Betty, follows his steps. They whisper in the backroom, show gesture to reject son' partner. Such manner is too cynical, she offends because slighted. She urges him to lead home. He tries to persuade, so she is patient. Though she is village woman, but she has self-esteem. She insists and utters the following sentence. If you are not willing to deliver me to home, I leave now. He doesn't want to lose a woman he loves; he turns the steering wheel and drives the car toward her house. They arrive, he sits for a while apologizing for his parents' behavior. She keeps silent but nods ahead. He leaves her with confusion.

He has set foot in the house. Father calls and suggests him to stay away from her. Father's suggestion makes him to bows sluggish, he is awry. If he rejects father's wish, he will be labeled as a dissident. But if he accepts it, he will lose a lover. This case makes him awkward and sad.

Since then, she was reluctant to meet him, she never wanted to visit his house again, but they still keep in touch. He asked her to lunch together; she rejected his call. On particular Saturday night, he contacted her by phone. On that occasion he intended to meet her at home, she minded. She gave a reason; she had a family affair. Be Tommy as an owl misses the moon, as vegetable without salt, he has an empty life.

He is sad, Mr. Henry none other than his biological father caused his sadness. She is nonchalant over his grief. Her mind is more focused on work to manage the famous capital mass media, Capital People Daily.

As a lecturer, she intends to educate the students to become the future generation. As Editor-in-Chief, she wants to continue to take part in suggesting an important and interesting news to the public. A bright idea comes up, she wants to unite the campus life by broadcasting task.

She meets the leaders of the National Television; they discuss her idea. Their decision spawns a new event suitable for students, it was entitled "Reality". This event is a talk show, a host is Elly. Reality is broadcast live on National Television and is housed on the campus of State Leading University. The show is for an hour-long; an event is filled with direct questioning and it sometimes invites famous figure as a guest star.

Today is Saturday at 09:00 am, The Reality begins. A woman named Yanty turns on the television, a channel she chooses is National Television. She soon hears students' voice hanging out on the simple stage. Before the event starts, a host comes. She introduces herself, her name is Elly. Yanty unnerves when seeing a host is a woman with tapering eyebrow. An audience now is surprise waiting for what Elly does.

The team which resembles this event is brilliant. To increase the event more lively, the opening broadcast invites a guest, she is female activist engaging in human right. The seconds later, a woman comes up to the stage. She is short-haired woman wearing a yellow shirt, trousers and glasses, her full name is Sari Mutiara, she was called Sari. Be they are two heroines of nation hope.

Yanti doesn't move from the front of television. Elly begins with sharp, reliable and tickling questions but those are flowing as water in the river. With the style of a famous journalist, she begins an inquiry.

Elly asks, what prompts you to be active in human right?

Sari is sad and explains, my mother died the days after mass protest by students and society. Then, mother met journalist and explained the human right violation carried out by security force. The next day in the evening, mother died persecuted by unknown man. We reported this tragic event to the police. But, human right violation cases aren't showed. I was disappointed as a son, it so compelled me to follow field of law and I devoted myself as Human Right Activist.

Elly continues a question. What effort did you do to uncover that case?

We have contacted the Commission on Human Right and they forwarded our hope to the Attorney. We are waiting for solution, but no bright news we get.

What do you think the mother?

Sari weeps and says as a daughter I never forget mother. We were intimate and treated us as a friend.

What are your hopes for future?

Sari tells, we hope that government works to uncover the case. The law should be enforced in country we love.

The questions were asked by Elly on human right defender. Here is last question.

Elly asks Sari a closing question. What is your advice to students?

My suggestion is that students who are next generation should never weary struggle for human right. They, so, learn the law.

After completion of an interview with the guest star, now the students ask Elly. The arising question is on her history. The first questioner is a woman, Tety.

Miss Elly, who is your full name and how many comrades do you have?

My full name is Ellysabet, we comprise three people; I am the eldest son and both my younger brother are men.

Please tell me your education?

I graduated from State Leading University, then continuing the study to Australia and taking a higher degree in broadcasting from the University of Sydney, shortened Usyd.

Tety asks on Elly's marital status. I got a news saying you were not married why?

Elly smiles for a moment, then she answers, no man interests me.

The answer invites laughter, an audience shouts. A student comments. How it could be possible no one wants, you are nice, famous and you have a bright future. Another student interrupts. Elly, if you don't mind, I introduce you to my uncle. Are you willing? The campus is jarring caused by a ridiculous student. An event is closed before the sun stings the skin.

A first Reality show is festive. Although the show was over, students still cluster to discuss, they promise to attend on next Saturday. A student determines to ask friends. The same wish comes from artists, they will present on next Saturday.

No one can deny the event echoes here and there. Public are interested in engaging in talk show led by Elly. In the second time is planned to bring high official of a state as a guest star. People know him clean, honest and his education is law.

Who won't want to see Elly? Yanty turns out graduation of Faculty of Economic of State Leading University, she is one idolizing Elly. She is interested in joining on The Reality event held by her university.

The next event occurs on Saturday in the second week, Yanty and neighbor attend the event, they arrive at the gate of campus. The crowd inhibits car's speed. A passenger turns out Elly, she is being asked by fans to take picture. Yanti at first wants to do the same, but because visitors are queuing, she delays a wish. Awaited moment arrives, Yanti is standing next to Elly, she shakes hands and takes a picture with young leader welcoming and friendly. Yanti is as having a dream.

Today's event is conducted on time, it begins at 09:00 am. Elly interviews chairs legal institution, Arnold, a moment after sitting on a chair. Besides telling hobby and his plan after retirement, he believes law enforcement is key to fixing the nation. Because law was not enforced, then legal violations occurred including rampant corruption. When she asks the human right issue, he argues human right violations were caused by ignorance of organizers of state on human right. As a result, they tinker without ever realizing what they were doing was wrong. The other errors were caused by arrogant behavior. The powerful party argued truth depends on strength they had, they acted against weak party. She interrupts and asks him on his meeting with one of the litigant. He explains that he has met Powel. Powel asked so his party will be won in a matter being handled by the institution Arnold leads. Powel even promised to transfer money associated with the corruption case. But Arnold rejected Powel' hope, and he asked Powel to leave the office. Interview with Arnold is closed with a question related to his plan after retirement. He will return to hometown where he was born and works as a farmer.

The third week of The Reality show is filled with Guest Star of State official in charge of education. He is Charles Thomas holding position of Minister of Education. He is scheduled to spend cheerful Saturday with Elly and students. The minister will present fifteen minutes before the event starts and he will direct dialogue with students.

Minister keeps promise, he comes on time. The seconds before the event, he stands in front of students. The photographers perpetuate his presence on campus known to be haunted. Elly is now in action, the interview begins.

Good morning Minister, are you healthy?

Yes I am, he replies.

Ready to receive piercing question?

He laughs and replies; I am ready one hundred percent!

She continues, public' opinion says, the change of curriculum creates project for corruption, your response?

The opinion is wrong! But officers were taking an opportunity in smallness. Here, they were doing corruption; they have been brought to justice

Many people complain because the cost of higher education is expensive. Your comment?

Minister explains, expensive and cheap is relative. But for achieving good quality of education, a large cost is required. It is accepted, expensive car, for example, needs high production cost.

Time to speak with Minister comes. Debriefing takes place in an atmosphere of emotion. That day a mother named Maria presents, her son studies at Faculty of medicine. She expresses lament on Minister the cost of education is troubling herself. Since her husband died, she relied on small business, selling used clothing for paying tuition of the son. She is worried that her son will drop out of study. A silence occurs, Minister is speechless, other attendees could not hold back tear, tear of sadness. Minister then encourages Maria and son to continue to achieve the goal. If she finds obstacle related to tuition fee, government through Ministry of Education will offer a scholarship. Thomas reminds students to keep studying hard to achieve a goal and never forget to do a favor to parents who have bothered to pay for a son. Before leaving campus, Thomas is asked to sign a plaque as a token of inaugurating new building of Faculty of Medicine.

The Reality program held at the State Leading University is the third time for Elly in collaboration with National Television. An expected time arrives; that is debriefing with Elly. A student asks what challenges she has ever experienced. She tells at length challenges faced during her career continues. She doesn't forget to tell a saying that goes, higher the tree faster the wind, higher the position, greater the challenge. One of big challenge she has ever experienced is slander. A wonderful occasion is used to share experiences with students. She says, talking with students is a picture of her love for the next generation.

Nineteen

A success of Reality results in new thinking. People give advice so the show is expanded. They hope the show no longer takes place on the campus of State Leading University, but expected to be carried out on other campuses. People argue, a host has a key role to make the show festive. Elly is a woman on stage which runs the show. So, they suggest the program is changed into new entitle, "Elly Show".

The parties support the plan. First step they do is forming a management team consulting with relevant parties. They contact prominent entertainers and an university leaders are in lobbying. They collect opinions and materialized. The show has a change. The broadcast time is no longer on Saturday morning but shifted to Saturday Night. A management argues, Saturday night is a holiday for students and others, so they expect the event will be more festive and crowded.

Something unexpected happens, launching the event is postponed. Circulating news says mutation on Elly to be done. What new position she will handle, nobody knows. The society knows shifting of her position from news in newspaper. Newspaper says, Chief Editor of Capital People Daily will be transferred soon. Issue says she is still in charge of the group of company. A reliable news says, her mutation will take place this week. A successor graduated from Faculty of Letter of the university in capital. An official at the National Television is coming up on television, he is Director of Broadcasting. He announces she is transferred from Chief Editor of newspaper becomes Chief Editor on National Television. This transfer is related to the success of Reality program. Based on a survey conducted by National Television, the show was interested in people. This could be showed by advertisements airing during The Reality show takes place. So, her mutation is a promotion. Congratulation for you.

The Reality show has changed into Elly Show. A newer edition of Elly Show takes place at Main University of People, it locates in another large city in heart of state. Elly's presence is graceful, she is as King's daughter. She is wearing black pants, a white shirt, and gray vest. It is well with her smooth skin and tall body. She doesn't just inspire students, but she presents graceful step, as the step of the famous model. She comes up in the multipurpose building. The first show is more lively because enlivened by three singers of capital top artist. Students take part, they launch fireworks into the air. The glitter of fireworks then decorates the sky at night.

Elly is an icon of the event, she begins an action. She gets a chance echoing National Anthem. Her vocal is melodious and clean as vocal of Gloria Estevan. Her tone is high, nears tone of singer Whitney Houston. An entire audience applauds to hear.

A theme of Elly Show now is Students for Nation, it presents local officials and executives. One of whom is Governor of State, Mr. James King. The event takes place relaxing but peaceful and wisdom. Great men express cases, we make these as lesson. How they achieve success and without ever tired of doing the best for the beloved country. As a regional leader, King is asked to express an opinion on students. This local official turns out a graduate of Main University of People. When he is asked to speak, he claims to be proud of an alumna of Main University of People. He advises that academics continues to improve education quality thus becoming one of university giving birth to honest and clean leaders and they serve people.

Another audience is Mr. Patrick, consultant of Human Resource Development. He expresses the following message to students. Students are struggling together to enforce the law. If law is not running well, then injustice will occur throughout the country. The country can thrive if law is enforced as fair as possible. Let us together create a seamless way to be enjoyed our grandchildren. The chair of alumni forum, Mr. Romulo, is invited to speak. He is an association of alumni of Main University of People reminding a whole range of academics to build nation together.

First episode of Elly Show invites students taking to stage. Elly asks impression and messages as a student. A student, Thomson, studies at Faculty of Law, now he is entering the sixth semester. As a law student, he believes same as people, law is disappointing. Law enforcement officers violating the law make people irritated. If we want people know law, it should be meted out to them severe punishment. We hope, law enforcement officers understand his opinion.

The event is closed by delivering books to students taking on stage, Elly does it. On the front cover of the book is written, Changing Fate of the Nation. The book content tells how to manage country well. Here, a leader must realize nation's goal according to statute that has been planned.

At the closing ceremony, a well-known musician group is requested in action. Students go up on stage, they are dancing to music echoing. Once music stops, students rush shout, they are satisfied.

What is news to Elly Show? This time is second episode, coming up on a campus of High School of Publication. The campus finds on waterfront of a state. The stage is in the Main Building with capacity of 8,000 people. Event's theme is the leader of Anti-Corruption. Elly goes into action to lead talk show. This graceful woman opens the show with a light joke of the typical student. She then continues by calling guest star, he is prominent anticorruption, Purnama. By the local language, Purnama means full moon. She at glance says why he was called Purnama. When his mother was pregnant, she watched new moon. The light could light up earth's surface. His mother hoped her fetus when an adult was willing and able to open the path of light for anyone who took darkness of life. The entire audience applauds her explanation.

Everyone knows the person named Purnama, he used to be called Mr. Pur. His role in the fight against corruption makes his name popular in the society, he often comes up as headline news. This differs from state officials which people say they are synonymous with corruption. He is known as honest, clean, transparent and generous man. Generous epithet attached to him because he often grants for people needing help.

At debriefing session, questions arise on how he can be different and he runs on an honest way. The question that strikes is, he shows clean behavior for the sake of larger purpose. He proves that such an opinion is wrong. The following is an interview conducted by Elly at him.

You are known honest, honesty is a main base to be trusted to others. How can you do?

Don't lie, once we lie, it will continue to next lie. Keep silent is better.

What makes a man honest?

Your question is easy to answer! our society is religious men. Faithful people should fear of sin. Lying is a sin.

Please tell us a more reason?

Assume that lie is embarrassing and disgusting

How to keep honesty?

We train a behavior not to lie. Who loves a lie he is a swindler.

Linkage of lie with corruption?

Keeping a lie can make someone into a villain. Corrupter is a right villain, it bothers people.

Can you describe a brief tip so a person doesn't corrupt?

Never think to have an object belongs to someone else. The corrupted money belongs to people.

Purnama further describes at length a lie. He suggests we imagine the face of people to be lied. Lied people will show a sad face, they will be disappointed and even anger. If such facial expression is directed to the person who lies, then he will be uncomfortable. Lying affects and undermines one's life until the end of life. If people around us don't believe because of lies we do, then we will be ostracized. Lying is as a rotten carcass. Even we try to shut, people smell odor. He says more opinion. If you want to be honest, you should gather with honest man. Never hang out with liar or cheater because later we will become criminal against humanity.

The third edition of Elly Show is held to welcome Independence Day. The theme is Saturday Night with former President. Event is planned well, so special and different from an earlier events. Elly Show organizes various events and attended by more than 10,000 students from various faculties. Elly Show is held two days, each day lasts for two hours. An event is held on the campus of its trademark is a yellow jacket, International University.

An interactive talk show presents popular guest star, and he has proven to lead the nation, his name is Harry. Before the host and key person present, the engineering team represented by Edward, invites the audience to stand for a moment and to sing a national anthem. Elly then invites student's voice. An audience is cheering and clapping, awaited man comes up soon. Mr. Harry is coming from the back. The students sitting cross-legged on the basic floor stand, they welcome former President and give way to him. Mr. Harry is with Elly on stage laid out very interesting. A former high-ranking official with the nickname is Mr. Har greets an audience most of younger generation. Conversation begins. Students are given an opportunity to ask questions. A spectacled woman called Tin begins questions.

Mr. Har, you have visited institutions, your visits were unannounced, what is your purpose?

Government employees should be disciplined and they must be ready to serve in time. They have liability as they have been paid by society.

Was your way successful?

Yes, it was sure. Officials were caught absent transferred, employees violating the rules were delayed to move. Vice versa, excellent employees were rewarded.

Mr. Har is accused of hard by employees given sanctions, what do you think?

I am a person who loves others because it God's command. Human should know a duty. A wise man is one who puts duty than right, it does not reverse.

Tin later asks on handling a street seller. Another question she asks is the fate of workers whose fate is full of confusion. She asks the last question.

Mr. Har, what is main need of a leader? The former president says, the most important case one should be clean, honest, and he becomes a good example for people he leads.

Elly asks Mr. Har to carry message and impression to students. The following is an explanation. Our beloved nation can compete with other nations if the younger generation will lead the nation with honest and clean. A leader must love people. Love is so nice because God gives it to people. No love is nicer than the love given by God. Keep love and not tainted with selfish sense. If someone is wrong to give love, then it will hurt his self. Thank you.

Mr. Har is known as a leader in loving people. Over his love, he is called by students as Professor of Love.

Elly's action on International University now sends the message to students. She urges them to keep honesty, don't violate law, and they must prevent from doing corruption. She says our country is rich, we must manage our wealth well. Important message she delivers is not to waste the wealth we have, those are for greater interest, nation interest.

She talks the sweet experience which was unexpected. That was whenever interviewing key people in this world such as American high official. But she says valuable interview is not only to interview high-ranking official. She tells her work strengthens spiritual experience when she was interviewing a victim of the human right violation. A woman who was born 28 years ago says each interview has a different impression.

The talk show is hypnotizing thousands of students. The whole audience is entertained with interesting style of the famous band. Students are enjoying Elly Show that becomes a young intellectuals pride.

As delivering valuable information for young generation, this event attracts new talent interested in working as a journalist. So, The committee holds competition to read news in front of television camera. One hundred and fifteen participants are taking part. Five of best people read news. Assessment is based on quality of script to be read. The best one is won by a man named Bertony. He looks stunning and hopes to work as searcher or reader of events that occur in the society. For his achievement, he gets a scholarship to continue studying at university in Australia.

At the end of the event, Elly, a close call of Ellysabet calls the following names. They are outstanding students. One is Pieter Jacob, he is a Faculty of Engineering student who developed information technology at Robot. As one of the excellent students, standing ovation greets when the name Jacob called. Other names called are Noris Johan Van and John Stanley. Elly show is closed with a speech by Rector of International University.

Twenty

Elly's age is now 28 years old, her love story with Tommy finds new history. His father changed stance, he was ready to receive her become daughter-in-law. Father worried over son's behavior. Since Tommy's affair with Elly was not agreed, Tommy was daydreaming, irritable and he often locked himself in the room. His behavior has been taking the weeks, and it has no signs of changing for better.

Father hears phone conversation of the son with a friend. Tommy is told to come to a discotheque and he will receive drug supply. He leaves home at 21.00 am, goes to the promised place. Until the next day, he has not returned and his cell phone is not active. Father is afraid of something unexpected happens.

Next day, father finds out where a son. An evening after dusk, he goes to the discotheque, a place where Tommy promised, its name is Single Man Discotheque. Visitors are crowded, he doesn't find son. Father is panic, stress, and he returns with disappointment. Something unexpected happens, a traffic accident. Father suffers broken bone and needs surgery. Father is brooding at hospital, he corrects himself and realizes an accident is caused by vanity. He is guilty for refusing Elly on base of a villager. He turns and asks Tommy related his love with Elly. Tommy says, it freezes.

Tommy does a trivial way, let trivial case who knows he takes a happy news. From the hospital, he tries to contact Elly. He presses the button matching to her number, no answer. Voice message says phone could not be contacted and asked leave a message. He does it, the following message is left. Good day Elly, I am now in the hospital accompanying father because of the traffic accident. Please contact me. His hope has not been signs of pleasure, his massage is not answered. He sends more message. The sound of the answer says sending a message is still pending. He bows sluggish on chair wondering when she activates the phone. His wait for news doesn't last long because he falls asleep on a chair. He wakes up when someone opens the door of the room where his father is treated. She turns out hospital nurse on duty. The nurse is checking father's health. The result of examination shows normal heart rate, blood pressure is good. She finds different in body, father has abnormal body temperature. Tommy stays in the hospital from morning to evening. His mind is split in two, thinking of father's health and waiting for phone news from her, he disadvantages. When he leaves the hospital, what she does is still in a question mark.

The Pleasant news comes, time shows at 11:45 am. She contacts him and inquiries the health of his father. He is in the house; he answers his father still has not recovered and father should be in hospital the more days. Elly, we are better to meet in the hospital alone; he appeals to that single woman.

He arrived at the hospital first, followed by Elly ten minutes later. They meet at the gate of the hospital. He shows sad face and shakes her hand. Your phone is not active, you might meet? That is right, she replies. She tells more why she didn't activate the phone. In addition, there was a meeting, she was busy preparing a new program with friends. They have planned, it should be launched at coming month.

They step toward room 301 where the father is treated and they stop in front of the door. He opens the door and meets two people. She is a woman named Betty, none other than Tommy's biological mother. The another is a man, Mr. Henry, Tommy's father who ever applied cynical on Elly. She comes in and embraces by Mrs. Betty. Their meeting is emotional, she and Mrs. Betty show same expression, a deep sadness. I am sorry Elly, Betty says sobbing.

Mother's cry wakes dad. He blinks to see a woman. With full of doubt, he asks, are you, Elly? He gets up from sleep and shakes her hand. Then, he says nothing, grieves and sheds tears, tears of regret.

People admire him because he is successful, an entrepreneur, and has much money. An achievement he reached makes him conceited, he rejected Elly as a daughter-in-law. A traffic accident makes him conscious, it causes he is lying on the bed. During this time, he is rich in treasure but poor in term of morality, even he is poorer than a beggar moral. everything has changed, arrogance has turned into wise behavior. He is in tears; he apologizes. Elly, forgive me for my conceit so far, that is the sentence he says while patting her back as cues accepting her. She crushes, she forgives prospective in-law. We hope, tomorrow is better than today.

Mr. Henry returns home after the days in hospital. He experiences a lifelong disability. His step is abnormal, he is limping. He cannot stand, let alone walk. He must use a crutch, wheelchair and he must be accompanied by someone. His health has not recovered, he is still being carried on walking.

Intimacy between Tommy and Elly meets new chapter, a love story is wider, they run more real love. They are often alone losing in love as a love story of Adam and Eve. This world belong to them, others ride.

Today they are lovers, they are close and united. Closeness never produces quarrel, let alone to cause conflict. Selfishness has gone, emotion has gone too. They are understanding and belonging. A love they run can be described as a love story between Romeo and Juliet, wonderful.

On Monday she leaves work at 20:30 pm, sits in the living room, takes the phone and connects it with the mother. She advises so mother comes to capital. This wish she has never done. If she had something important, she returned to the village. She is busy; she doesn't have time to visit the village. Mother understands, she comes the next day.

Elly at night expresses to mother the new job she has to do, she wants to cover news to abroad. The explanation is not finished mother interrupts. Do you want to visit war field again? You make mom upset. Does your company have an employee who can replace you? Listen mom, who was sent was the meeting's decision. We are teamwork, other employees help a course of coverage. Mother further asks, can the plan not be postponed? I think you marry first and then you leave. It is impossible, news will be stale soon. Mother resigns and says your job is up to you, but don't forget to pray to God. Mother bows, tears in eyes, she is concerned for daughter safety.

On a Saturday night, Elly invites Tommy to come soon. She wants to tell an important message. He comes with flowery heart because he knew her mother was in capital. His view says, what she will tell is regard to marriage. He arrives at the house after sunset. Suspicion arises, she doesn't appear as usual, throwing a smile at the start of the meeting. This time, she steps with a serious expression. What message she wants to tell? He asks. She tells a plan, she will make special coverage related to piracy which often occurred in a sea of Africa. So, she will visit African continent soon.

He followed a piracy case in black continent; it was cruel and sadistic. He sighs, and he is worried she could be unfortunate. If she died while performing the duty, he could be a widower before marrying. It means their love story will end. But for the sake of duty, he lets her departure though with a heavy heart. He comes home and his heart is wrapped with sense of worry. May God bless her trip.

The night air is cool because blown by the breeze. He is brooding in the room and he doesn't tell it to parents. Drizzle adds loneliness that night. His gaze is empty leads to a room wall, and he hopes pure love shines again to adorn his days with her.

Rain continues, even more heavy. Night air might understand what he feels, so it feels sad and dripping rainwater. Wall clock has shown at 22:00 pm, the sky is so dark because of rain. Without realizing, he falls asleep in the room.

In the morning before leaving for office, his father asks. Tom, how are Elly? He bows, takes a long sigh and tells as follows. Listen, daddy, I was shocked when meeting her. She told me within the days longer she will travel to Africa; she intended to make special coverage related to piracy often took place. I was worried because a herd of pirates never hesitated to kill hostages if their demands were not met. When I asked her the risks that might occur, she told me a light answer. Die while covering news has been an occupational risk for any journalist. With a heavy heart, I had to let her go. Dad asks again when does she go? She will go soon, she may does it this week. Dad is silent, he understands son's concern and bows head. Dad suggests, we leave it to God.

Tommy was born and raised from wealthy family, but he has never felt the true meaning of love. Love of a lover who will fill his heart throughout life. He has felt it after making love with her. So he is hopeful, love with her ends in an aisle. The love story is now tested because her lover will leave him for days.

One day before departure, he visits her to the house. He intends to deliver loyalty waiting for her until returning to the homeland, live or dead. He brings a red rose; a symbol of his sincere love. Before leaving her, he says my love for you won't stop even if this red rose has wilted. He is playing love pattern of Cinderella style united with the story of Ugly Betty. Eyes are a mirror of soul. His eyes are stunning and they show sign of affection, she is fascinated. She convinces he loves her.

Goodness should be rewarded goodness, a poem is replied a poem. The same is applied to romance, love is replied with love. Love doesn't ask, it gives. She motions for him to come closer. He steps, he embraces and kisses lover's forehead. Bye honey! Such is a short sentence he utters.

Twenty One

A long time ago a teenager ran strange love proverb, because love, task is abandoned. Time changed, proverb was out-of-date, lovers left it. She is a smart woman, adolescence has been gone through, now she is mature. Love proverb being operated is more modern, love should be left for call of duty.

She is never afraid of death, she will visit dangerous zone. People called it dangerous because in this place vicious pirates were often in action. It locates on Africa peninsula. Target crime is aimed at ships, and pirates have squeezed ships owned by large companies.

Her purpose to visit a malignant region is to make a special report on the events of crime that happened. The plan, she will interview a pirates leader. Other staffs will help her duty in doing a course of plan. She and friends leave using foreign aviation plane. They land in one of Africa countries; it was called Simali. They arrive in Simali at afternoon around 16:30 pm; they stay at hotel. Visitors are black skin men, but others have white skin tourists from Europe. Hotel security reminds her, a plan should be canceled. Because he says, pirates are dangerous and immoral. They make everyone hostage. An important goal for them is getting much money.

Risk has become part of journalist life, she continues with plan. They go to destination using special car which allows car's wheels moves on pothole. During journey to destination, they find no interesting scenery except wilderness growing on earth' surface. Then weather is cloudy, wind is blowing hard. A strange sight occurs a kilometer before arriving at destination. Road is blocked with sticks of wood. This case causes the driver slows a speed and stops the car. The atmosphere is quiet and dark, a weather is cloudy. They want to know what happens. She and friends get out from the car, surrounding people come closer and surround them. She is happy because she thinks they soon get help. Joy changes into worry. Then, residents carry a firearm. Don't move! One of them snarls. He approaches her while brandishing a gun ready to shoot. A man turns out to be a pirates leader, his herd calls him Big Boss, he is fluent in English. Elly and friends are ordered into car, they then disappear swallowed by dense forest. They stop at the site of confinement, its neighborhood resembles military barrack. Men are using military uniform, others are not. Boss calls and asks her on what a goal and aim. She says she is a journalist intending to make special coverage of piracy that often takes place in Simali. Shut up you, Big Boss barks. We are not pirates but freedom fighters. From surrounding environment and their brief conversation impresses they are fighters. They show unfortunate behavior; they are not polite to journalist.

Big Boss calls her and says, if you want to survive, please tell your superior so he provides a sum of money as soon as possible. She complies with the demand but asks to be given an opportunity to communicate. A Boss agrees, she is welcomed to do.

Government is shocked, officials debate and arising disagreement on how to cope with the case. They argue a government should play a role. Opinions arise, an official considers this case is not government's responsibility, but a responsibility of sending institution. The debate shows to no settlement, a trend is to the dead end. President speaks, orders officials to do possible ways to make sure the safety of hostages. Compromise is reached. The government takes responsibility rescue while sending company bears cost demanded by pirates.

Negotiation with pirates is carried out with involvement of International Red Cross. Both parties agree the need, pirates demand ransom of USD 5,000,000, - The number is agreed on, its surrender is gradual. First phase of USD 500,000, - held when pirates release hostages and a part of ransom will be paid when hostages have reached safe location. Government represented by International Red Cross reasons an important problem is hostages safety. Official considers, that demands are met when hostages have reached safe place. Pirates object, renegotiation is run.

Hostage crisis by pirates is not to end. Latest information released by television states pirates pose greater cost. They know Elly is famous journalist. So they make her as primary reason of negotiation to increase demand. A representative for pirates delivers it from location of confinement. The weeks earlier, they have shot dead a hostage from an Arab country. Action they did, so the world knows they wanted to free hostages if their wishes fulfilled. Another victim was a Japanese man, Tabe Suky, was executed by shooting in the head until his brain scattered.

While negotiation takes place, government is trying to figure out to the countries where their navy is heading or near sea of state Simali. Within 24 hours, good news comes from South Asian country, India. Then an Indian Navy warship is passing near sea of Simali. Ship controlled by captain Prakash is ordered to be closer to beach Simali. Final agreement is reached, she and friends are released in the middle of sea, on rubber boat supplied by pirates. While ransom delivery is little changed, half is paid when hostages are in a rubber boat, while the rest will be paid when hostages have arrived at safe place. Time-release is planned in the morning at 08.00 am. Toward the mentioned time, Indian state-owned ship approaches in which two passengers representing the Red Cross. One is Philip, and another one is Tony Lee, they take part to save hostages. Ten minutes before 08:00 am, two speedsters drive to agreed location. Rescuers have been waiting for ship that will bring hostages. The sea now turns into limelight of news searcher.

Tense moment arrives. Hostages, employees of National Television, are transferred to rubber boat. Lee and Philip descend from ship. Lee hands over ransom, while Philip notices hostages. Philip shouts, where is Elly? He asks other hostages who have been on rubber boat when pirates reverse direction. A crew called Berlin shouts to call Elly, pirates didn't release her. Bangs sound, Indian Navy's soldiers open fire toward pirates. Pirates fall into the sea, others surrender, and Elly survives. Money is taken back. The whole crew goes up on Indian Navy warship. They are then moved from ship by helicopter.

A rescue spreads to homeland. Mass media makes a rescue as headline on front page. A reporter, Elly, becomes topic of conversation in society. People argue, she never gives up duty in dangerous zone because she is still single, she cannot mate.

Story of exemption is declared a success, but it still leaves questions. News related to her is confusing. A news stated she was still being held hostage. Another news said she had flown into the homeland. This makes Tommy confuses. He is curious and wants to take part to the airport to pick up his girlfriend, but he doesn't get a right news. For more precise information, he hangs out in front of television.

The latest news comes from television station where she works. An important message is sent, she survives. Truth of news is supported by broadcast images showing she is being interviewed by journalists. She returns to homeland the next day and is scheduled to arrive at 09:00 am.

Tommy's wish to go to the airport is strong. He leaves from home in the morning at 07.30 am. Journey takes an hour, he arrives at airport at 08.30 am. He is amazed at crowd of people; they are journalists. The employees of National Television take part in coming up to airport. They wear uniform complete with characteristic color of hat, blue and white.

The crowd squeezes; it looks as she comes. And, she steps up to exit. Step halts intercepted by journalists, she is interviewed, questions are answered. Last question, when do you get married? She smiles, I hope soon.

He doesn't meet her, but he is happy to have seen a lover's face. He lets she leaves the airport by office car. Then, he follows her group, leaves the airport and goes straight to home.

The next day she lives press conference. Her duty acts as an interviewer, this time she comes up in front of television as interviewee. She tells reporters her experience during a captive. The first night of confinement, she occupied a slum room; it fitted inhabited by homeless. She slept on plywood using a mat, a room smelt musty and full of mosquitoes. A pirate gave her a glass of water in the morning, and she enjoyed simple meal at 13.00 pm. He gave reason their country was poor, so they could not give proper food for people. So, hostages had to undergo same fate as Simali people, taking potluck.

On a second day, a man fluent in English interrogated her at length. He knew she was famous journalist, pirates made her as a great asset to raise bargaining power. So they increased demand. One time, pirate asked her look at hostage. His condition was sad, he was tired and sluggish as malnutrition person. Pirates did such, so she feared and relevant institution obeyed any order they wished. When rescue team didn't meet their demand, she could not bathe; it caused she couldn't sleep. Then, her eyes were closed when dawn was breaking. Because of lack of sleep, she was asleep and woke up when a member of pirate pounded her room and yelled out. They said, I was brash, and I was a buffalo.

A thrilling moment arrived at last day. Pirates brought and asked her and friends up to speedsters ready to go. Heart was beating hard because she was separated from friends, a pirate asked her to move to different speedster. Separation was carried out because pirates planned to withstand her and they will demand greater ransom. But, we reached middle of sea, liberation happened and it was ended.

A reporter asks. Do you give up to be journalist? I continue to cultivate journalist's work until end of life. Life and death depend on Almighty. Last question, do you have boyfriend and when do you get married? I have a boyfriend. If God blesses me, I will marry at once. Thank you.

An interview in front of the screen was completed, now mother interviews.

Elly, do you still want to charge in the dangerous region?

Job I worked is not my wish, but a call of duty.

I heard you have a boyfriend?

Yes mom!

What are his name and occupation?

His name is Tommy working as an Entrepreneur.

If you are comfortable when do you introduce him at mom?

Elly answers, I try as soon as possible!

To complete an answer to the mother, she further describes who is Tommy. A brief history of a young entrepreneur is as follows.

Elly knew Tommy when she was in university. He enrolled in Faculty of Economic majoring in Accounting. When she was still at first year, he often teased her. The buildings where they underwent learning were in near place. She never responded his temptation because she realized he was a rich man. His father was a big businessperson engaging in office building while she was a villager who was innocent and she didn't know people's life in capital. Further information said, he was a slow figure, often too late go to campus because he woke up late. His poor habit made him to be called by friends Buffalo. Above information made her to keep distance with man who while a student looked neat.

They never communicated; they met at a wedding. In the day full of wisdom, he came up as an entrepreneur of entertainment, while she attended as a guest. He was single, and he hoped if she could be made an as life companion. Since then he often called her until he visited to her house. That was a new phase of important moment they blossomed, she became interested because he has changed. He no longer was deserved title of buffalo, but he turned into hard worker.

Twenty Two

That is fact, love is life need. Man needs love and woman does same. They later marry to complete each other, and both coexist. It looks incomplete if someone doesn't have a partner. Task to complete with life partner has approached to Elly. Besides following mother's expectation, her age is enough, she is 28-year-old woman. Tommy expects to have wife and children, his parents hope grandchild.

Love story opens a new chapter, the day is Monday afternoon before dusk. It is still in working time; she calls him from office. She asks when he has a time to meet her mother. If you want to introduce me to your mother, I will try as soon as possible. Wait the minutes, I will call you back.

He is busy, office tasks must be completed soon. The first task is receiving guests who intend to use his company to fill entertainment at the marriage ceremony. Other tasks are preparing cooperation contract and signing agreement document. He completed the duties before going home. Then he calls her. Hello Elly, how are you, my dear? He asks her wish to introduce him to mother-in-law candidate. She once repeats a question.

When do you have spare time? My mother is still in capital, I intend to introduce you.

Tommy is happy. He answers, okay, I do it today. But I am going home first because my body is full of sweat.

Well, I am waiting for your presence tonight, Elly replies. She then disconnects phone with him.

He never meet mother-in-law candidate, so today is a historic moment in his life. An interesting style is a need for him, he comes with a typical dress. He believes, mother-in-law candidate doesn't hesitate to accept him. A gift as cake is carried on, the goal is that the mother is respected. To support his showing so he comes up more convincing, he sprays perfume into body. He sets out to use a private car without no worry his presence will be rejected. When he arrives, he displays good impression, smiles, and bows as a sign of respect. He says good evening mom, and he lends a hand for a handshake. Mother may seat him. He introduces his name is Tommy. There is a gift I bring for you, he hands small parcel he is carrying. She smiles and receives. She asks questions.

What is your profession?

I do my work alone.

What do you mean?

I have own company.

What business do you do?

My business engages in entertainment.

You are great, young but you have own business.

Tommy laughs, my work is a small businesses.

Mother asks the last question. Where did you first meet Elly?

He explains they have acquainted when both became a student at State Leading University. He was more senior, lectured at Faculty of Economic. Explanation continues on work he does and a story of his other duties. She is happy to hear. His history is seen coming from good family. Mother welcomes him to talk with daughter and steps into the living room.

That day he works full-day, so body is tired. He no longer spends much time with her. Before rushing home, he intends to invite mother for dinner together. He asks Elly when the right time for that purpose. She suggests being fulfilled before mother returns to the village. That is a good suggestion, they agree the plan will be conducted the next day.

He keeps a promise, comes before dinnertime at 18:30 pm. Mother is a villager, he knows what food she needs. He directs a car to nearby restaurant, people know it, its name is Executive Restaurant. Besides providing modern spicy food, it serves the typical food suitable to a villager. Thus, food is served as mother's taste. A restaurant's employee comes to meet them, she brings a list of menu dishes. He takes it and lets mother chooses the favorite menu.

Villagers have a different appetite with city men. Mother prefers natural food than modern spicy food. She chooses grilled chicken and soy sauce as the flavor enhancer. Tommy and Elly order different menu from the mother, they are more interested in modern cuisine. Now they are waiting.

They talk cases as family problems, work, and plan for future life. Conversation stops when ordered food is served. Mother says the meal is delicious and still warm. A stomach is hungry, they eat the food. This restaurant serves full menu. Besides main menu ordered, at their desk are available extra menus as bananas, watermelon, and mango. They enjoy them as dessert.

The dinner was finished, he motions to call waiter. A woman approaches him and hands list of the bill. He takes out a wallet, surrenders a Visa credit card and signs a bill. They leave the restaurant after meal account is paid.

Where do they go after that? Do they go back toward house? The answer is no. He wants to make mother happy. He directs a steering wheel toward a park. Local Government calls it National Monument Park. In the middle of park stands National Monument, a symbol of local state.

Visitors are crowded. They stop at the humble stall, they no longer wants to enjoy tasty food, but order a soft drink. Mother orders hot tea, Elly wants avocado juice, while Tommy asks hot coffee. He creates a sweet sense of family.

Surrounding the monument looks lights of building twinkling. They show a glitter of metropolitan atmosphere in capital. Night dew adorns an air, a natural cue marks time over at 21:00 pm. Mom is old, she cannot resist cool night air, and she proposes to go home. They return when the atmosphere of park is still cacophony filling the nightlife.

His first approach is undeniable to leave good impression for mother. This signal can be shown when she wants to leave the village. He comes up with the purpose of delivering her to the railway station. She says I am happy to see you. When do you visit me to the village? He replies, if I have no work, I see you to the village. We hope, it happens soon. When she steps into the train, Tommy shakes hand with her and attaches an envelope containing money. She asks, What does it contain? That is to buy sweet tea and lifting a bag containing clothes belonging to her. Congratulation and welcome to destination.

He has a green light from the mother. This makes his spirit increased. He is never moody again, but on the contrary, his love is more flowering. He never wakes up late, leaves an office on time and the work is completed according to schedule. When finishing an office task, he no longer visits other places but returns home. He wants to prepare a new life.

Their behavior is as poem is replied with poem. After Tommy faced mother-in-law candidate, now Elly does the same. She wants to get closer to Father-in-law candidate, because of his father is not healthy. She calls him and asks father's health. He tells at length his father is still with a cane to walk. Father is more improved to do physiotherapy. She asks time to visit; he proposes on Sunday afternoon.

They want to meet at 12.00. He picks her up to house and they go to a restaurant, intend to get lunch. The next trip is to his house, it finds in luxury residential, its territory is known Fancy House. The income of people living in Fancy House is more than average. Most sons and daughters ever received higher education abroad and they become an entrepreneur. Even as an employee, they work in foreign private company, because they want to earn high salary. This place has value added, it locates in capital's heart, be equipped by good and smooth public transport. Shopping center and shops are available. Means make surrounding people can fulfill daily need.

He stops the car in front of the fence; they get out and walk to home. His mother, Betty, is cool to water flowers in the garden, she sees them. Betty ceases to do a work and welcomes their presence with the following sentence. How are you, my daughter? Elly smiles and shakes hand while saying, I am fine. She is welcomed to seat while Betty steps into the kitchen to ask to be supplied drinking for Tommy and Elly. The father, Mr. Henry follows to the terrace where Elly and son are. An emotion is going on, Elly is treated as daughter. There is Tommy's younger sister named Yessy. She has had a close relation with Elly; they joke. Yessy throws question, Tommy was facing new mother-in-law, is it right? Please to be honest! They laugh. Tommy admits, yes you are true a hundred percent. His parents and Elly laugh again. The familiar meeting creates an atmosphere as if Tommy and Elly have married.

The next day Tommy expresses to parents an intent to visit the village, he wants to meet with mother-in-law candidate. Father and mother agree and ask when the time is. He plans next week, calendar shows national holiday. The day is a religious holiday; it falls on Monday, so he plans to leave on Monday morning. On Sunday the day before, his mother, Betty, asks if he is ready to the village. He answers okay then asks if his mother has a message to be carried. Betty wants to send nice regard to Elly's mother. Another message she adds if the time comes, we will visit together to the village. Good moral support.

An evening changed to morning, this morning falls on Monday. He leaves from home to lover's house. She is waiting, a dark bag lies on the terrace, it has daily wears. He is no longer out of the car, instead; she gets and brings her bag into the light green car. He puts a plastic bag in the backseat. She sees it, then asks what parcel has. He says, a black bundle has apples, these will be handed over to her mother.

Most people use holiday as a day of rest, others use for recreation. This time, holiday has own particularity. People stay at home at religious holiday, it causes street is quiet. They reach village fifteen minutes faster. Her mother has heard that he with daughter, will visit the village. Over the plan, mother is ready waiting for prospective in-law.

Mother is familiar with car driven by him. Four-wheeled car now passes by and stops. Mother gets up from seat, rushes to open the gate. They get out, walk to front of home. A moment later, she and her mother engage in an intimate embrace, while he shakes hand with mother the seconds later. Mother, what is up, he asks to begin a meeting. She replies, I am okay. He hands the apples, then they sit on front terrace talking many cases while enjoying nice flowers growing in the park. Elly interrupts, red flower is as first red rose. He smiles, remembers red rose ever given when she went to Africa. The red rose has been withered, but he proves his words; he is still loving her.

Sun shows prowess stinging living creatures on earth's surface. They don't realize when time shows at lunch. He asks family to a restaurant serving local typical food. It comprises rice, grilled chicken and fresh leaves as a vegetable. Waiter serves them well, she puts fruits on table as an extra food.

He wants to leave a good impression for mother-in-law. After lunch, they don't go straight home but go around the city visiting the entertainment place. They agree to stop off at the local cinema, Studio Twenty-One, comprising six theaters. It means they have six options; they chose family drama movie. After watching a movie, they go home and talk for a moment. Since late afternoon, he says goodbye to mother-in-law and back to capital with her. He drives a car; she is tired; she sleeps during whole way.

Three days later parents calls him. His mother suggests he marries to her. He doesn't mind and even agrees with parents. A new idea comes, meet between both families. He and she discuss; they take an agreement, a meeting will be held in village. Besides relaxed atmosphere, its location away from hustle and bustle can create an atmosphere more familiar. They suggest an idea to parents of both parties. Preliminary agreement is reached, but they look for the right day when the meeting takes. Based on the data listed in the calendar, a national holiday is on Friday of first week. They decide meeting is held two weeks later on Saturday the next month.

The meeting is exploratory stage; it doesn't involve relatives, involving a family member of both parties. He attends with parents and younger sister while she accepts his family with mother and siblings. At the meeting, her mother introduces herself as Mrs. Thomson. Thomson is the name of her deceased husband while her real name is Louise.

She and mother intend to create a sense of family harmony. They host his family with lunch. Menu is simple but encouraging for healthy living. There is no meat, side dishes include sea and freshwater fish. Vegetables are still natural, those are fresh local vegetables, they include young and fresh foliage. His mother, Mrs. Betty, comments as follows, menu is delicious. It creates mild laughter from a prospective in-law candidate. Her daughter, Yessy, interrupts. Mother later in capital must offer more delicious dish, please not talk only. They burst out laughing. Due to laugh, his father stops enjoying a banana. He says my daughter is right.

The meeting results in good impression, both parties become communicate often. Onetime Betty was doing phone connection, while at other time, Mrs. Louise was calling a prospective law. Mrs. Louise tells an important idea, the wish to meet again. Mrs. Betty and family receive it. On that occasion, Mrs. Betty agrees the meeting will be conducted at their house.

Time goes so fast, plan of the meeting is two days away. Mrs. Louise, with her brother, Jefry, visits capital, they stay at daughter's house. The house which locates in street Independent is now occupied five people, Elly with two younger brothers, mother and uncle Jefry.

Familiarity is real, Elly's family is picked up by Tommy's family. His family comes by using three cars parked on the side of the road. They form three groups. The first group is a couple getting married soon, Tommy and Elly. The second group consists of parents, Mr. Henry, Mrs. Betty, Mrs. Louise and Mr. Jefry. Being the third group is young people, Yessy with Elly's younger brothers. They then go hand in hand toward Tommy's residence.

They arrive at home around 11:00 am. Stomach is not hungry, bread is served, enough to fill stomach and duodenum. They sit in the living room, talk past and future life. Talk continues, they focus a conversation on Tommy and Elly. Conversation stops when lunch time arrives.

As a family of an entrepreneur, they don't do kitchen work; they order catering company which prepares matters on lunch. Three employees are ready to serve for power lunch. The menu presents dish village; mixed with food with seasoning modern. Now they are free to choose. Enjoy lunch together.

Meeting they do is not only a reunion or family gathering, but produces a new agreement. They agree that Tommy and Elly must be married; the plan is next year.

Twenty Three

Since Tommy's wedding plan with Elly was proclaimed, they have nothing preparation. She is still, as usual, working with no mental load. Her emotional tie with him is running well, they find nothing.

After three months passed, the first step is done. He is asked on marriage with her. He and she counsel to make sure when talk between families begins. They agree discussion begins two weeks later.

A country they were born has tribes, its society comprises cultures which differs one another. Tommy comes from ethnic Papa from the eastern region while she comes from ethnic Jaba representing western hemisphere people. The indigenous case becomes an important issue in wedding procession of east people. Both families keep marriage procession is held under his indigenous family.

Today is an early stage of marriage according to Papa Indigenous way called Tonggo. His family sends messenger that acts as an ambassador for family to negotiate when marriage proposal is done. An interesting and tough discussion happens when the meeting takes place. A conversation is as conducted by two high-ranking officials of two countries, each side shows greatness. Time has shifted but custom is still used as weapon to assert dominance.

Tommy descends from Duke, he expects big wedding ceremony. They want custom used is Papa because they want to show they are successful large family and they come up as a King descendant. But her family objects. A luxury way is inappropriate and excessive, they should find a meeting point. This leads to create fun and exciting discussion.

Agreement on prevalent marriage has a heavy wedge. Papa and Jaba society have a different habit, it becomes a serious problem. He and she undergo the ordeal, they are worried not get married because of differences in custom.

A Papa leader expresses an opinion. Though we differ in custom, the marriage must run well. He suggests a saying, man bears while woman upholds. This term points out cost load to be borne by each party. Bear is more weight than uphold. It means man bears the greater cost of the wedding. Both parties agree. Marriage is celebrated with man's custom, most of wedding cost is borne by man's family. In addition, wedding execution need not be massive.

An appointed day comes, his family visits her house in the village to applying. The application is a procession to ask her willingness marry to him. On this occasion, his family wears a reddish color uniform. They bring a symbol of premarital as cake, fruit and another form of gifts. Her family prepares a dish for honored guests. The application is received then both parties do stronger bond, ring exchange ceremony. She is a journalist and chief editor of a television station, so journalists come to immortalize wedding proposal. News says Elly soon marries to Tommy. The next step is to discuss date of wedding, reception place and cases related to wedding. For urban communities, dating marriage is based on availability of building for wedding reception and a day off so whole family can attend to event without sacrificing too much time. This differs from ethnic communities Jaba. Marriage is sacred and holy procession so it should choose a right time.

His family realizes culture embraced by Jaba people, so deciding the date of marriage is handed over to her family. Date of marriage is postponed because they are waiting for notice of indigenous council Jaba.

Last issue is how many invitations they spread. From a family of groom proposes 4,000 invitations while bride's family argues 2,500 invitations are enough. This has nothing significant problem. An agreement was reached with a plan to spread 3,000 invitations.

Day keeps changing and determination of date of wedding is getting urgent. Mr. Jefry takes initiative to represent family. He gathers indigenous people and they discuss to decide a niece's wedding day. Gloomy month according to calendar of ethnic Jaba is avoided for wedding. People believe, wedding in gloomy day should be avoided. They consider gloomy day is disastrous because dry season, emerge many diseases and drought.

Another case to consider is date and day of birth both prospective groom and bride. Under Jaba's calendar, combining day of birth cannot be underestimated to give blessing and happiness for groom and bride. If this calculation shows disaster, death and disease, then marriage is better avoided. To overcome this case, they select a better day. A good day under Jaba's calendar is a blessed month, it falls on the first week of December. Custom board meeting decides the date of marriage falls on December 5.

As in other society and culture, wedding procession on Papa society doesn't allow a bond of affection between man and woman, but it brings together two great families. Each party is busy preparing for the wedding. Family tie that has drifted apart because of social problems is reunited through marriage ceremony.

A man driving force of her family is uncle, Mr. Jefry. Whole relatives are invited, they gather at Jefry's home. Important issue they have in mind is place of wedding party takes place in future whether in the village or in capital. Wedding date has been entrusted to bride's family. So, the groom's family should be entrusted to decide wedding place. They argue, need to be wise for a smooth wedding. This decision is delivered by Mr. Jefry to Tommy's big family. Mr. Henry and his extended family accept this decision with pleasure. And Tommy' father tells that wedding will be held in capital.

Since determination of date and place of marriage, she is complete as a woman. She finds a partner who will spend time alone with her at happy and sad. Getting married is a dream of every woman including her. So, don't be surprised if she has owned wedding dress design.

She feels as to be struck by lightning, gets news her mother experienced traffic accident. The mother was hit by truck and was serious injury. An unfortunate event happened at the time mother completed family gathering at her uncle's house. Elly leaves capital and rushes to the hospital. Her arrival is late, the mother is dying. She regrets, condition doesn't give her a chance to take care of the mother. What mother experienced was God's will. Mother's body has now become pale, cool and stiff. A beloved figure dies on her lap. She cries, does nothing. Mother is a lost guardian, is gracious and merciful. She is sad, such figure has left her forever. Mother wades through this life with a solid determination and patience. Such properties are shown after Almighty called her father. She salutes mother; she doesn't have a chance anymore to repay mother's kindness.

Wedding plan turns into the funeral ceremony, this sad day is attended by thousands of mourners, taking place in full of wisdom. Most of those present are neighbors, relatives, and office friends. Tommy's family presents, they follow funeral procession until finished.

Most mourners leave cemetery when closing prayer led by pastor completed. She lays a wreath at grave of dear mother, followed by Tommy and other visitors.

Tombstone has separated her and mother, but mother will be in her life. She regrets no time to give grandchildren to the mother. But regret doesn't make mother back to her. What remains is sweet memory, this is unforgettable during her life. She is sure mother has been happy in Heaven. I am sorry mom, goodbye dear mother.

She doesn't work; she is still in the village. A sadness comes, she and siblings are orphaned, they occupy a house 25 meters of the riverbank. Most residents have gone wander around somewhere, this case adds to loneliness. She looks at a small park in front of the yard, that is a favorite place where mother spared time and watered flowers growing there, a place that made mother happy. Park is filled with flowers contributing various colors, the beloved mother made it wonderful.

Oh my God, why this happens, I could not stand. She steps to shady tree, her favorite place several years ago thinking her boyfriend when she was in high school. The wedding is postponed for a year; she is still a virgin. That status makes her be known as Village Virgin.

Printed in the United States
By Bookmasters